Every surfer's dream...
...A Secret Spot !

Secret Spot is set in a small Northern California coastal town, and revolves around the camaraderie between three young friends who surf there.

The young band becomes discontented with uncivilized surfing crowds, and inner city attitudes that pervade their sport and threaten to change their lifestyles.

They receive a message from strange, ethereal messengers and consequently take up an obsessive quest for an elusive place where waves are plentiful and fun is the rule.

They travel up and down the California coast and have a great adventure. However, the boys soon discover that the *Secret Spot* is much closer than they ever dreamed...

SECRET SPOT

by
Michael E. DeGregorio

BigWater Productions - Ben Lomond, California
(DeGregorio Productions)

First Edition,
First Printing - November 1996
Second Printing - February 1997
Third Printing - August 1998

ISBN 0-9649417-6-7

Edited by Janet Moore
Author Photo by Mark Berkowitz
Cover Illustration by Michael E. DeGregorio

For information address:
BigWater Productions
394 Bahr Drive, Ben Lomond,
California, 95005
Phone/FAX (408) 335-0229
Phone (408) 335-2696

Published in the United States by:
BigWater Productions - Michael E. DeGregorio is a publisher of written and video productions in the United States and Japan.

Printed in the United States by InPrint Corporation

Acknowledgments:

A special thank you to my son Mikey, whose picture graces the cover of this book, my daughter Sarah and her beautiful daughter Hayley Rose, my editor Janet Moore, my artist friend Denny Dederick for the wonderful black & white illustrations, my nephew Christopher Oliverio for the endless manuscript copies, Deborah Hanson for the great vitamins, Janice Weaver for her incredible insights and creativity, To Helen Ho and Triet Leary of M&P for the great computer graphics, and to my good friends at InPrint, Deepak Varshney, Paul Conn, Dennis Rubalcaba, Karl Winkleman and Dick Nelson. God bless you all.
Thanks for the trust, patience and assistance.
I love you guys...

...and especially to
my beautiful wife, Olivia,
who makes it all possible.

FOREWORD
by Janice Weaver

Many, if not all surfers are blessed with a moment, an instant in time in which a confluence of details, of tides, of friends, of personal growth, creates a fully developed image of their "ideal". This moment emerges for different surfers at different times, for the devout, perhaps many times under a variety of conditions. It is deep within the soul of a true surfer to unconsciously seek this convergence of elements, to capture this personal ideal again and again.

Michael DeGregorio's latest book, "Secret Spot", embraces this theme, and captures a sense of both innocent youth and underlying goodness that combine to create a true camaraderie. Not only has Michael created this environment in print, but it is a world in which he lives, has created, and openly shares with others.

Supported by his network of family and friends, and most essentially his wife Olivia, "Secret Spot" has come not only from Michael's creative forces, but from his courage. In writing, he has chosen a new path for himself and changed the course of his life by following his love of the ocean and his love of life.

He writes heart-felt descriptions of surfing that surfers can relate to, whether it be in a recollection from the past or a dream for the future. He provides a sense of history for the sport, and characterizes what is important to be passed down — not materialism or localism, but what Michael himself feels is the true essence of the sport — sharing the experience with others, and embracing camaraderie as an absolute. "Secret Spot" is a primer, of sorts, as to the joys of youth and surfing.

Compared to Michael's first novel, "Thunder Bay", "Secret Spot" has a more playful tone, while maintaining a sense of magic and spirituality. In it, Michael's richly textured descriptions transport the reader to the steep glassy face of an early morning wave, to the aroma-filled kitchen of a best friend's mom, to the fog shrouded glow of a late night beach campfire. And though the images are of surfers, written by a surfer, "Secret Spot's" appeal is universal.

Michael writes to remind the reader to look within oneself for truths and goals, but to not overlook the here and now – to celebrate the everyday, and to acknowledge and appreciate the details. He knows that the convergence of details that creates one's personal "ideal", that moment in time that is self-defining, is not limited to surfers. A laugh in the sun with a good friend, the soft smiling face of a sleeping child, the quintessential pizza combo on game night, can all be defining and significant and invaluable. Details can always add up to something wonderful.

As long-time friends of Michael, on land and sea, my husband, Wingnut and I rejoice in supporting Michael's creative endeavors. We look forward to sharing many more unexpected pleasures with Michael and his family, both in and out of the water.

Janice Weaver

Janice Weaver is an accomplished graphic artist and has been surfing for 10 years. She and her husband, Robert "Wingnut" Weaver, star of "Endless Summer II", "On Safari To Stay" and television, reside in Santa Cruz California with their faithful dog Sheila. Janice is an extremely creative person and just recently began the creation of her first child, which she and Wingnut expect in the Spring.

THE DREAM

Michael Anthony danced across the smoldering hot sand. His bare feet accumulated heat like batteries collecting a charge. Sprawled around him were hundreds of sun worshippers, baking in the late-morning sunlight. The musky stench of disparate brands of suntan oil blended with the pungent odor of the sea, and hung heavily in the air. When he reached the water's edge he broke into a sprint for the last several yards, then launched into the water. As the surfboard hit the water he jumped to his feet and stood upright. He slid over the shimmering surface. After a few yards he moved into a prone position and began paddling.

The blinding hot morning sun simmered down through the silver-green ocean surface, creating a tepid layer of water about two feet deep. Michael paddled along, thrusting his arms deep beneath him and propelling himself forward in gentle spurts of fluid motion. His motions disturbed the colder water below, causing it to swirl up to meet his fingertips.

He paddled along in a straight trajectory over the shimmering, glassy surface. When he had reached a predetermined point, he slid his legs down over the sides of his surfboard and immediately halted his forward momentum. He sat up and slid to the rear of the board while firmly gripping the surfboard's rails. Then he began to rotate his legs in opposite directions. This motion created an underwater vortex that pivoted the long surfboard from its tail in a sweeping clockwise direction. He was now in a headlong position perpendicular to the approaching wave. He began to paddle, matching his speed and pitch with that of the wave. Suddenly the wave moved underneath him and he felt the elevator-like lift as he was catapulted up its vertical face. He reached the crest and was pitched violently forward and down. Startled by the wave's force, he glanced over his left shoulder and observed the translucent wall as it became blue-green against the bright morning sun. Suddenly the wave began to mutate, growing larger and more ominous. Michael blinked his eyes nervously, squeezing them open and shut.

"No!" he thought, "It can't be...it just can't be!"

Michael jerked himself upright and began a fifteen foot vertical free-fall. The momentary feeling of exhilaration from the drop vanished as he gazed toward the beach. There, casting out ahead of him, a cobalt blue-gray shadow spread into the calm inner waters. Again, he craned his neck around and gaped in terror. The wave had transformed hideously. Its crest loomed menacingly above him. He swallowed hard.

"It must be at least thirty-five feet," he thought in panic.

His stomach turned nauseous as he peered down and realized that the wave was bottomless. Wind and water rushed violently up the sheer face and began to drive him upward. In moments he found himself trapped under the hollow crest. The wave enveloped him as it threw out, carrying him over the falls. He free-fell for several seconds until he struck the flat waters of the trough. He hit with a terrific jarring splash, skidding several times. He was unable to penetrate the slick surface. Then the turbulence pulled him under and began to tumble and turn him as though he was inside a commercial washing machine. He was drawn into a deep, dark abyss.

Darkness smothered in on Michael and he was about to succumb to panic and exhaustion. Suddenly, he began to hear the soft melodious sounds of Hawaiian music. The cold dark waters swirling around him gradually began to give way to blues and greens, streaked with shafts of yellow sun light. Michael's head burst through the surface and he began to gulp the fresh salt air into his lungs. In the next moment he found himself crawling limply out of tepid water and across a dry, blistering hot sand beach. The white sand was pristine and pearl-like and squeaked under the weight of his hands and knees. As he crawled along a dark shadow fell across his path. He raised his drooping head to see a mysterious tall dark man with a broad white smile. He looked Hawaiian. Michael gazed at the strange man. His face seemed vaguely familiar.

"Who can this man be? I know him. I've seen him before. Why can't I remember his name?" Michael asked himself.

Three more men advanced toward the tall dark man, and stood at his side. Michael quickly scanned their faces. They, too seemed familiar, but his eyes were quickly drawn to the third man. There was something almost paternal about this man. His face was shadowed by a large-brimmed straw hat that made it impossible to discern his features.

Michael stood upright and the hot sun beat down on his naked head and shoulders. He turned to face the ocean as the four men grabbed their surfboards and raced down the beach. They paddled out quickly. There were no large rogue waves now; only chest high waves lined up far as Michael could see. The men were soon laughing, hooting and cheering each other on as they rode wave after wave.

The tall dark man rode what appeared to be a very old surfboard, possibly redwood. The others rode sixties-style longboards. The four men were surfing alone in idyllic conditions.

"How can this be?" pondered Michael in amazement. "Why isn't there a huge crowd at such a perfect break?" As he watched, the sunlight suddenly became white hot and the beach flared and bleached away. Images of sienna and azure blurred his vision, then exploded in a blinding electric flash.

"Whooff!" gasped Michael, as he opened his eyes with a start. He lay for long moments in the still air of his dark quiet room.

The dream sensations slowly dissipated as sounds and muted colors continued to swirl around him.

"Yeah," he mumbled sleepily, "that's the way surfing should be!"

As his eyelids again grew heavy, he could still hear the ocean waves softly crashing, the laughing and the hooting.

Friends Surfing

It was a crisp, clear, windless day in Santa Lina, a classic summer morning. The rising sun cast brilliant bands of golden light over the black silhouette of the lower northern California foothills. Nick Giovani's white Chevy truck was stained tallow gold as it sped south on the coast highway. At five-thirty AM, the road was deserted. Nick, Michael and AJ gazed toward the ocean with anticipation, observing the long lines marching in from the southwest. It was a solid six foot swell. This was shaping up to be a classic morning for a surfing session at Private Beach.

Private Beach was one of their favorite breaks although it was anything but private. It was a quarter mile long impeccable white sand cove, protected by high cliffs on three sides. It was usually warm and sunny there, even on windy days. The solid rock reef, azure waters and conspicuous absence of kelp made surfing there a real pleasure. Even a moderate southwest swell there would produce some of the most perfect three to five foot waves on the northern California coast.

In the early sixties, Private Beach was the exclusive property of the local residents of the beachside residential area in Santa Lina called East Cliff. At that time the neighbors had gotten together and erected a chain link fence and gate with an oversized chain and lock. Each resident owned a key as part of the association and the only way an outsider could gain access was to make the long paddle from Wild Hook Beach to the north, or Casaligna Pier to the south. Through the years the fence fell into disrepair as the East Cliff area became a bedroom community for busy young families who commuted daily to jobs in Silicon Valley. Soon the gate disappeared as access was established by the steady stream of surfers and beachgoers who stampeded down the rickety stairs.

Although Private Beach was a mob scene most days of the summer, it was far enough off the beaten path that a diligent surfer could initiate a dawn patrol and sometimes enjoy uncrowded conditions. Dawn patrol was what a serious surfer did. It meant rising in the dark well before dawn, driving to the surf spot of choice and paddling out before the sun was even close to breaking the horizon. There, he would wait for first light and hopefully get a few uncrowded waves to him or herself. On most occasions, however, as the sun crested the low foothills, the boys would see other silhouettes bobbing around in the water just yards away. Apparently the word was out regarding dawn patrols. It seemed that there was just no escaping the crowds when it came to surfing.

After a hasty parking job and a quick change into their wetsuits, Michael, Nick and AJ scurried down the stairs and made the short paddle outside. They sat bobbing in the lucid waters, hoping that they were alone. Soon the sun began to fill the shimmering waters of the quiet cove. Yes, they were alone!

The three friends began dropping into one perfect little concave peeler after another. They surfed Privates for well over an hour by themselves, but soon a steady stream of surfers began making their way down the steps. The scene would soon transform into a typical crowded day at Private Beach. They tried to ignore the inescapable.

Nick took off on a medium-size wave. When he reached the bottom, he leaned way over until his face almost touched the glassy vertical wall. Then he set the longboard on its edge. His legs flexed as he transferred his downward momentum into the inside rail of the board. The board snapped around, transferring his kinetic energy into linear speed.

He pumped the board once to increase his speed, then pulled up into the pocket of the wave. Deftly, he stepped back on the tailblock and stalled. As water gathered beneath the surfboard, it created a kind of back pressure and lift, much like the effect of wind rushing around a wing. The board buoyed up and Nick began walking, one foot over the other for the entire length of the board – nine-feet two inches. He stood on the tip now in a classic toreador posture; head cocked jauntily and all ten toes curled over the nose. As he cruised along other surfers hooted excitedly and shouted encouragement. He finished the ride and kicked out with a flair. He paddled back out into the lineup and met up with Michael.

"Man, that was a beautiful ride, Nick!" said Michael in falsetto. "I was watching you from the water line. I wish I'd had a camera, it would have made a great photo!"

Michael winked at Nick as he clicked an imaginary camera in front of his face. Then AJ paddled up to his friends on his six-foot four-inch Billabong thruster.

"That was a beaut' mate," said AJ with a playful look, "You do amazing things on that barge of yours."

Off to their right and slightly inside sat a group of angry-looking teenage boys who had just paddled out. They bobbed in waist deep water with their arms folded defiantly across their chests. The morning sun glinted off the tops of their shaved heads.

The leader of the band was an older, large boy with a permanent scowl. His expression twisted the features of his otherwise handsome face. Suddenly the leader bawled out loudly.

"Too many f—kin' longboard geeks out here!"

His lackeys chuckled in harsh, machine-gun like bursts. When the leader saw that Michael was observing them he scrunched up his face.

"F—kin' longboarders!" he spat.

Again his lackeys responded by emitting simian- like grunting noises, like chimpanzees showing respect for the dominant tribal male. Michael's jaw muscles began to tighten up as he mentally prepared for what was shaping up as a possible altercation. AJ quickly jumped in.

"Hey, no worries mate...ignore those Agro's. They're not worth the energy," he implored.

Michael's jaw muscles flexed visibly as he paddled for the next wave. He caught it easily and began riding. Meanwhile, AJ turned around and paddled toward the takeoff area near the unfriendly pack. As he paddled he immediately turned into an approaching wave, lifted gracefully and dropped in. By now, Michael was paddling back out after completing his wave. He slowed his pace as he watched AJ begin his ride.

AJ was a native of Queens, Australia. He had moved to the United States after a summer visit in 1991. During that time he had met up with Michael and Nick. They bumped into each other on a particularly crowded three-to-four foot perfection day at Malibu. To AJ, it seemed as though Nick and Michael were the only two there that day who were really having fun. Their overt friendliness immediately attracted AJ.

Surfing at his home break in Queens had become too serious. It had taken the fun out of the sport for him. Meeting Michael and Nick on that day of surfing had been the deciding factor in AJ's decision to apply for permanent resident status in the U.S.

AJ was twenty-two years old and stood about five-foot ten. He was built solidly and when you patted him you could feel the sinewy strength in the muscles of his back and shoulders. At the age of fourteen he nearly lost one of his feet in an accident in a produce warehouse where he worked after school. A forklift dropped a large crate across the instep of his right foot, crushing it flat. The doctors were ready to amputate it, but at his mother's urging the team of doctors managed to fuse it back together. On land, AJ was a bit awkward and tended to favor that leg when he walked. However, once in the water AJ became fluid and graceful. He was left-handed and surfed backside, or goofy-foot, as it is called. His full name was Aloysius Jonah Mac Cray and it was real easy to figure out why he preferred his nick-name...AJ.

AJ hit the trough of the vertical wall, dipped back, bent his rear leg and cut a big wide turn. This maneuver threw out a big fan of water and squirted him straight up the crest of the wave. Now he moved the shortboard up and down the long wall in a roller coaster fashion that intensified his speed and movement exponentially. He climaxed the ride by smashing off the lip of the wave and free floating through the air for several feet. He landed on the trough of the wave with a surprisingly small splash, then kicked out.

Michael was impressed. As AJ went by he caught his eye and gave him the high sign.

"All right, AJ!" he shouted.

The shaved-head leader watched Michael and AJ. His face contorted again.

"Hey, Helgy!" he yelled, "Why don't you and your kook friends go home!" The obnoxious wisecrack was followed by the predictable cackling of his toadies.

Michael felt his jaw muscles tighten once again. He was barely resisting the urge to smash the brainless idiot to smithereens. Nick had

overheard the comment. He paddled over to Michael.

"Don't pay any attention to them, Michael," said Nick.

Michael turned to face him.

"Doesn't that crap bother you?" he asked.

"Yeah...sure," replied Nick, "but I feel sorry for those losers."

"Sorry!" snapped Michael.

Nick's eyes softened and his face became somber.

"Yeah, sorry," he replied, "cause they don't understand the true magic of surfing. The great feeling you *should* have when you're out here."

He held his arms up and craned his neck as he scanned the area. "In the fresh air, surrounded by the ocean and the waves!" Then he looked at Michael and AJ. "Surfing with your friends and having real fun!"

Michael considered Nick as he observed the shaved-head gang.

"Humph! I'm sick of their friggin' attitudes. They ruin it for everybody!" he spat.

"Hey, bud, how long have we been out?" asked Nick, attempting to change the subject.

Michael looked at his watch. "About 3 hours," he said.

"Uh-huh...I'm hungry!" said Nick. "I think I'll take the next wave in. It's getting too crowded anyway."

He grinned, turned his board and began paddling for the next wave. Michael folded his arms and watched his friend.

"Right behind you, buddy," yelled Michael.

He watched Nick ride all the way to the sand and smiled in admiration.

"Each surfer has a certain grace of his own...even those agro jerks," he pondered.

He shook his head then turned his board around. With two strokes he was in the next wave and rode it straight in.

Michael trotted up to Nick who was already standing beside his truck, changing. Nick was balancing on one foot, pulling the thin neoprene wetsuit from his body. Steam rolled off his skin as he peeled the suit down to his knees.

Michael removed his towel and clothes from the car. 'Towel changing' is one of the more mundane but absolutely indispensable surfing rituals. It is a quickly learned skill and something that most surfers become quite proficient in, whether on a crowded municipal beach, the front lawn of an unsuspecting beach side dwelling, or teetering on one leg in the bed of a pick-up truck on a busy highway.

As Michael wrestled with his own unwilling rubber suit, he laughed and joked with Nick. They talked about the great rides, enjoying the afterglow that always follows a good surf session. They had already begun to put the unpleasant incident with the nasty bunch out in the water behind them.

Nick was completely changed and Michael was pulling his pants on. Nick walked to the edge of the cliff.

"Common AJ...I'm starved!" yelled Nick through cupped hands.

AJ acknowledged, holding up one finger, high in the air. This is a universal surfer hand sign that indicated he would ride just one more wave, then come in. Very seldom, however, is this signal given any real veracity.

"If you're not up here in 5 minutes, we're leaving without you!" yelled Nick.

Pleasure Cafe

The 1988 Chevy Suburban roared throaty as Nick down shifted the four-speed top shifter transmission. Surfboards moved around in the rear, reacting to the truck's forward momentum. It was a pure surfing vehicle, with everything non-essential removed to allow for safe storage of surfboards and gear. The only place for passengers was the front bench and Michael and AJ fought incessantly over the shot-gun position. The warm morning wind blew Michael's auburn hair across his face as he hung his arm contentedly out the opened passenger side window.

Nick decelerated the vehicle smoothly and purposely from sixty-five mph. With each gear change he raced the truck's fully blue-printed 350 engine to well over six-thousand rpm. He changed the gears, moving to third, then second and eased the rugged vehicle into the parking lot of their favorite roadside restaurant. As he turned in, the big mud and snow tires slid slightly in the loose gravel of the parking strip. He rolled up to the restaurant's big front window. The cafe's neon sign reflected down on the polished surface of the shiny white hood, *Pleasure Cafe*.

The Pleasure Cafe had the best food in Santa Lina. The service was good and the servings were plentiful; made to order for hungry young men fresh from a strenuous calorie-burning surf session.

They clamored noisily out of the truck and made their way toward the cafe's front entrance. Their path was partially blocked by an ancient four-door sedan, parked carelessly over the pathway. They turned sideways and squeezed between the low front fender and the newspaper rack positioned near the cafe entryway. Michael studied the automobile. A frown spread across his face. It was a nineteen seventy-three four-door Chevrolet Monte Carlo. It was faded silver gray, with patches of primer showing on the hood and fenders and with rust spots on the roof. The wide front end sagged low on a well-worn rickety suspension. This was the type of car that would cause him instant anxiety whenever he spotted one in his rear view mirror. It would usually be tailgating, then sway from side-to-side when the driver was finally forced to activate what was left of its brake system. Michael would hold his breath, fully expecting to be rammed from behind.

The boys entered through the cafe's front door, laughing and shoving. The front of the cafe was filled to capacity with its customary morning breakfast crowd. They took seats in the waiting area.

Across from the boys sat a young woman and her two children in a small booth near the front window. She was dressed in a royal blue business suit and was frantically scribbling into what looked like a steno pad. To her right sat her young son. He looked to be about eleven years old. He wore a long-sleeved dress shirt buttoned to the top, olive-drab jeans and brown oxford shoes. His younger sister wore a Barbie Doll T-shirt, faded blue jeans and high-top tennis shoes.

"Must be dressed for dayschool or the baby-sitter," thought Michael absently as he observed the trio.

The scene activated a memory from Michael's own child-hood. He was ten years old and his mother and father had just decided to separate. He felt adrenaline constrict his chest muscles as he recalled that day when his mother informed his brother and him that she would be leaving their father. He was standing in front of the oversized brick fireplace hearth in the living room of their two-story home in suburban Los Gatos, California. The tears that streamed down his cheeks quickly evaporated as he stared blurry-eyed into the heart of the yellow fruit wood fire. Michael remembered how he had turned to his mother and made a joke, pretending as if he did not care and strutted arrogantly away. He felt an old scar begin to reveal itself. The familiar hollow pang burned across his chest and arms and weakened his legs.

"This must be a broken family," he thought as he stared tenderly at the innocent faces of the two young children. The memories kept streaming through his mind. He recalled how after the divorce his brother, James, would try to tag along with him and his friends. Michael had been cold and indifferent, feeling uncomfortable with his younger brother's behavior. Strangely, ignoring James seemed to ease his own pain. He knew now, in retrospect, that he really wanted to hurt his parents, but could not. So James got his wrath.

He watched the young boy wipe spilled oatmeal from his sister's T-shirt and stuff a napkin under her chin. Michael lowered his gaze. More memories.

He recalled the day he discovered that James had grown up. Now they began to share common interests. He actually began to enjoy having his brother tag along. They worked together on Michael's 1953 Desoto, and took road trips and surfing safaris. They became real pals. About a year ago, James had joined the Air Force and was now stationed at an air base on the east coast. He had not seen him since then. His introspection was interrupted by a female voice.

"Please follow me," ordered the waitress, leading them into the overfill room in the back of the restaurant. She handed them each menus. Michael attempted to break his pensive mood.

"Hey, weren't you a stewardess on my Lear jet?" he quipped.

Nick chuckled nervously, always embarrassed by Michael's tactlessness, but AJ picked up on Michael's comment.

"Yes, me little Sheila...didn't we go to different schools together?" quipped AJ in a heavy Australian accent.

They all chuckled now and the waitress, who was accustomed to their antics, continued unaffected.

"Can I get you something to drink?.."

"Coffee!" they chirped in unison.

"And our usual," added Michael.

The waitress nodded knowingly and hurried off. Nick looked around the small room and noted that it was empty except for them. AJ lit up a cigarette. Michael began to describe in detail one of his more memorable rides of the morning. He utilized elaborate hand gestures, expressions and sound effects to indicate the size of the wave and the way it broke.

"Did you guys see that wave I dropped into? I did a big bottom turn, tucked into the pocket, stalled and then ran to the nose..."

Michael made an exaggerated, wide, sweeping hand gesture. As he swept his hand around he crushed AJ's cigarette. Half of the smoking weed swung comically from the part that was still in his mouth.

"Oops, sorry me little Aussie bloke," said Michael with fake sincerity, "but you shouldn't smoke those things mate...they get in your mouth!"

AJ picked tobacco from his lips and spit small pieces from his mouth. Michael ignored him as he continued with his story.

"I had all ten toes clean over the nose and I was still working the wave. Man, it was great!"

AJ probed the back of his tongue with his index finger, fishing for a particularly bitter particle of tobacco. He gave Michael a dirty look.

"Yeah, I saw that ride," said AJ sarcastically, "you walked the board, did a beautiful off-the-lip and a floater. Could you have done anything else on that wave?" AJ winked at Nick, then gazed with mock adoration at Michael as he placed his hands together under his chin, "Oh, Mikey, you are such a good surfer! You are my idol!" AJ made kissing noises.

Michael scrunched up his face in disgust.

"Did you guys see that five I got?" said Nick with a smug expression.

Michael chuckled. "Heh, yeah...you almost made it to the nose."

"If you were riding my board, you'd have made it to the nose," added AJ.

They all laughed, then Michael added, "If he'd been on that toothpick of yours he would have sunk like a rock!"

Michael chuckled and gave Nick a half hug around his shoulder. The waitress arrived with their orders. She began to move about the table, refilling their coffee cups.

"I hope you washed your hands before you put your finger in me hash-browns," said AJ, continuing the rib. The waitress ignored his comment. She hummed to herself as she filled their coffee cups.

All conversation stopped as they dug into the delicious food.

After a few minutes of silence Michael renewed the conversation, his cheeks bulging.

"Man, it was fun this morning, but it got crowded so fast."

He took another big bite out of his hamburger, chewed quickly and stored the food in his right cheek.

"I'll tell you what...I was this far," he gestured with his forefinger and thumb, "from punching that shortboard weasel's lights out."

AJ dropped a forkful of eggs and hash-browns on his plate.

"Whoa mate! Lets watch those shortboard comments...I'm one, ya' know."

Michael pushed himself back from the table and slumped over. He glared down at his plate as if he had suddenly lost his appetite.

"You know, there's got to be a place where it's not so crowded. A spot where there aren't so many jerks in the water."

He paused, looking first at AJ, then at Nick.

"Like in the dream I had last night," said Michael.

The boys continued to eat as Michael spoke.

"I had a dream about this place...and it was so real, so beautiful! You know...it had perfect surf, no crowds and no weasels."

He paused and looked thoughtfully.

"No wonder they were having such a good time."

AJ was puzzled by Michael's comment.

"Who's *they*, mate?" he asked.

"Oh, the guys who were surfing in my dream," said Michael absently.

"Hey...how about it?" he blurted suddenly, looking at AJ and Nick excitedly. "Let's go on a surfing' safari, whattaya say? Let's head down south and see if we can find some bitchen, uncrowded warm-water waves somewhere!"

AJ spoke up.

"But the surf is terrific here right now. Why go south?"

"Naw...that's not it," said Nick, "he just wants to try and scheme on some of those hot south coast chicks!"

Michael became perturbed.

"Wouldn't you like to get away from these crowds and maybe find some perfect little peelers all to ourselves?"

He nudged Nick and smiled.

"Something different."

Michael and AJ continued arguing the merits of going south vs. staying home. Soon Nick became aware of voices from a table directly behind them. This startled him slightly because he had not seen anyone enter the room since they were there. He chewed slowly as he peered over his shoulder. Three odd-looking characters were seated at the table directly behind them. Then, with his mouth in mid-chew and his head slightly cocked, Nick caught Michael's eye. He silently gestured toward the three men. Michael and AJ stopped arguing and turned their attention to the men. Michael found himself staring intently at the man with the wide-brimmed straw hat. The hat was tilted forward, hiding his features. Michael rubbed the back of his neck nervously.

"When did those guys come in?" he whispered to Nick.

The men sensed that they were being monitored, and lowered their voices. Realizing that eavesdropping was now impossible, Michael renewed his argument with AJ. Nick, however, was intrigued. He continued to try and listen.

Michael began nibbling French fries from Nick's plate. "AJ...Are you riding with us tonight?" he asked.

AJ replied through a mouth full of toast and jelly.

"Uh-umm." He swallowed loudly. "Naw, I'll meet you blokes there."

Michael now turned to Nick. He interrupted his concentration.

"Hey, Nick! What time do you want to go to that beach party tonight?"

Nick shook his head as if to clear his thoughts.

"Oh...yeah, that's right. Tonight is the party at Wild Hook Beach!"

He considered Michael's question carefully before answering.

"Well, let's see. About eight PM should be good. It's almost dark by then. That gives me enough time to run all the errands I promised I'd do for Mom."

Michael was satisfied with Nicks answer, so Nick returned his attention to the three men. As he strained to hear their conversation, Michael and AJ noticed and began to listen too.

The heavy-set man in a flowered Aloha shirt gestured and remarked to the thin, gray-haired man. "Yeah, Mason, those are some great waves," he exclaimed, "and the dolphins that swim through...leaping and playing! It's a beautiful spot, peaceful and uncrowded...the secret spot."

"More coffee?" asked the waitress.

The three boys flinched simultaneously and glanced up, embarrassed. They had not noticed the waitress approach. She repeated her question.

"Can I get you boys anything else? More coffee? Dessert?"

The subject of food always commanded their immediate attention. They ordered.

"I'll have some chocolate cream pie," said AJ.

"I'll have the apple pie," said Nick.

The waitress turned toward Michael.

"Rice pudding," piped Michael.

"Fine," she said, "I'll just be a minute."

She hurried away.

The boys resumed their eavesdropping, catching fragments of the men's conversation.

Their desserts arrived and she refilled their coffee cups. They dove in. AJ's features changed as his cheeks, stuffed with chocolate pie, began to bulge. Suddenly he scrunched his face in displeasure. He attempted to catch the waitress's attention as she moved about the table collecting dirty dishes. Finally he reached over and tapped on her forearm. She looked in his direction, expecting the worst.

"Scuse me miss...but I think the cream in me pie is bad." AJ chewed as he spoke through overstuffed cheeks.

The waitress eyed him suspiciously. She was used to their antics and was adept at handling them. She moved around the table and stood behind him. She remained there for long moments, scrutinizing the wedge of chocolate cream pie in question. AJ began to hunker over. He was staring straight ahead with an expression that resembled an anxious chipmunk, cheeks protruding with incriminating evidence. After a few moments she reached casually over his shoulder and slid the pie toward the edge of the table. Without warning she drove her index finger straight through the dessert, piercing the cream topping and the chocolate filling. Her perfectly manicured fingernail made an audible click as it struck the plate beneath the crust. She nonchalantly withdrew the digit, coated with sedimentary layers of whipped cream, chocolate and fragments of flaky crust. She moved it close to her face and examined it. After a moment she plunged the finger into her mouth. She hummed an unrecognizable melody through her nose as she allowed the chocolate and cream to melt over her tongue. Her expression was one of deep contemplation.

"Tastes okay to me," she reported.

AJ was flabbergasted. He sat quietly as a strange smile spread across his face. Finally he glanced at Michael.

"Bloody pie's sour," he mumbled defiantly.

The waitress's expression of indifference transformed to bewilderment. Without hesitation she launched the index finger again. It followed a predictable path toward the pie. AJ watched in horror as she scooped up a big dollop of cream topping, dunked it into his black coffee and swirled it around in a deliberate, counter-clockwise motion.

"Nope, not sour!" she announced. "If it were bad it would have curdled in the hot coffee...must be okay!" she smiled sweetly as she walked away.

AJ stared straight ahead, slack-jawed. Nick and Michael began to chortle. AJ looked at his friends. His face was flushing bright red, which accentuated his bulging cheeks. He turned away, knowing that if he laughed now he would surely choke.

Michael spoke suddenly, breaking the mood. "Hey AJ, where did those three old dudes go?"

They turned toward the table where the three strange men had been. It was empty. They had vanished.

For long moments they sat, unmoving, gawking at one another. Nick opened his mouth to speak, but was cut short.

"Whelp," said Michael, standing up and gulping the last coffee from his cup. He shook his head nervously and glanced at the empty table. "Take care of the check, would-ja buds...I gotta take a leak. Meet ya' outside."

Nick glanced at AJ, who quickly gobbled down the remainder of his pie. He stood and hurried off toward the front of the restaurant. Nick realized that once again, he had been stuck with the tab. His friends knew that Nick's family had money. His father had been very careful in his financial investments and had left he and his mother with a substantial estate. Nick was well-off, so-to-speak, and didn't mind picking up the tab for his friends. It bothered him, however, that they just assumed that he would always pay their way.

Nick popped the last bite of his apple pie in his mouth, picked up the check and headed out. When he reached the register AJ was waiting, reading a menu. Nick glanced nervously toward the back room as the waitress made change for a twenty. He returned to their table to deposit a two dollar tip under the sugar dispenser. He scanned the table where the three strange men had been sitting only minutes before, then shook his head, turned and left.

Beach Party

It was seven-thirty PM, when Michael and Nick pulled up to the dirt parking area overlooking Wild Hook beach. Michael eased his 1964 Plymouth Barracuda over the deep pot holes and root stumps. The car's heavy-duty suspension absorbed the uneven surface as he nudged it forward, to the very edge of the sheer fifty-feet drop off. Like a huge canopy, a two-hundred-year-old Monterey pine dominated the protruding cliff area. It's gnarled root system wove through the soft clay earth, surfacing and dipping throughout the dirt lot. In the diminished dusk light it appeared as if the tentacles of an ancient, immense octopus were about to seize them as they rolled forward. The ancient tree was probably responsible for protecting that portion of East Cliff Drive from the relentless erosive action of the sea.

They got out of the car and looked below. An unusual mist hung above twenty feet from the surface of the beach and skirted the cliff's edge. Through the strange fog they could see a bright yellow spot of light, presumably from a lone beach fire. The scene reminded Nick of an ethereal stage setting with a spotlight directed down by a phantasmal stage hand on a lofty perch.

"That must be the campfire," said Nick.

"Yeah," said Michael. "We could be early. Maybe that's AJ down there waiting for us."

They descended the steep trail and the wood staircase that led to the beach. Actually, the stairs were a new addition. Five years ago there was only one way to get to the beach. You had to scale the vertical cliff to a precipice. From there you let yourself down the last twenty feet on an old fire hose. The access was dangerous and many tourists and inexperienced surfers had been injured. Finally the county put in the treated timber and cement structure. This had transformed the once pristine Wild Hook into a popular party beach and the surf line-up became a zoo.

"I hope there's some good looking girls here tonight!" said Michael.

"You might get your wish," confirmed Nick, "there's supposed to be some girls here from school."

He gazed up at the clear, star-studded night sky.

"What a night! I hope that low fog goes away." He hesitated slightly. "But I'm really tired so lets not stay too long, okay?"

"Okay grandpa!" said Michael contemplating his tanned, sandy-haired child-hood companion. Michael and Nick had been friends for as long as either could remember. They grew up in the same neighborhood only five houses apart, went to the same school together and attended the same Catholic church. They were like brothers, which suited Nick just fine, since he was an only child. They were inseparable and even fought like brothers. No matter how strident a misunderstanding was, each would protect the other without hesitation from outsider attacks. Michael considered himself to be Nick's big brother and took it upon himself to protect him, though Nick would never admit that he needed such protection.

Michael was in deep contemplation.

"I wonder if Monica will be here?" he mumbled, half to himself.

Nick glanced quickly at Michael. His eyes twinkled. "You two hit it off pretty good during school, huh?" he said with a wry smile.

.

"Yeah, she's great!" Michael reflected. "I haven't seen her since the senior all-night party. It would be so cool to see her again."

He touched Nick's shoulder.

"There...the campfire's over there," said Michael, pointing. They hopped down the final steps of the stairway.

"Let's see who it is."

As they walked toward the campfire, they saw three men. AJ was nowhere in sight.

"Maybe we're too early...or I could have gotten the days screwed up," said Nick.

Michael did not respond. He continued to approach and inspect the three figures around the campfire. The pale yellow light illuminated their faces.

"Hey!" whispered Michael into Nick's ear. "Aren't those the guys from the restaurant this morning!"

Nick felt a shiver run through his body. He too recognized the men.

"Yeah, I think you're right!" he said.

The short hair at the base of Michael's neck began to prickle. He rubbed it with his left hand. They were only a few yards from the fire now as Michael addressed them.   "Scuse me you guys, but do you know if there's a party here tonight?"

The three men had puzzled expressions as they glanced around the deserted beach.

"They told us there was a party at Wild Hook," continued Michael, looking toward Nick for agreement.

The big, heavy-set man looked up at Michael. He was wearing a different Aloha shirt.

"Uh-huh," confirmed the man, indifferently.

"Oh...I guess we're early then?" asked Nick.

There was no response to Nick's question. The heavy-set man finally motioned for the boys to join them. Nick sat down immediately. The big man looked up at Michael, still standing. Michael slowly squatted next to Nick.

"Hey!" yelled the big man, "get these young hot-dogs a couple-a beers!"

The man with the gray sideburns pulled two beers from a cardboard carton and tossed them over the fire toward Michael and Nick. They each caught a can. Michael began instinctively probing the can top with his index finger.

"No pop-top?" he thought.

The top was seamless and smooth. He turned the can over and looked to see if maybe the opener was on the bottom. Nothing there either. He glanced at Nick. He seemed to be having the same problem.

Suddenly, the big man bellowed. "Need the church key?" he boomed. "Catch!"

Michael turned and spotted a silver object sailing end-over-end toward them. He caught the object deftly.

"Church key?" he asked with a puzzled expression.

The men roared with laughter.

"The boy doesn't know what a church key is for!" bellowed the big man. "What's this generation coming to?"

The men roared again.

Michael clinched the metal device into the lip of the can and leveraged it upward. The can made a sharp metallic crack.

"Sssss..Ka...Pap!"

He flinched as the agitated beer began to spurt skyward; he quickly raised the can to his lips. The frothy beer forced its way down his throat where it expanded, came back up and sprayed from the corners of his mouth and out his nose. He lowered the can. Beer spray arched out toward Nick. He dove for cover. More good-natured laughter burst forth from the men. When their laughter and Michael and Nick's expletives died down, the men began to relate stories about their personal adventures. It seemed like a well-practiced ritual. Each spoke in turn. The man with the large-brimmed hat, however, sat silently as he had in the restaurant. Michael again found himself studying the man. Occasional, when the fire flared, he could almost make out his features.

Now the big man began to testify that surfing is the greatest sport on earth, but even more wonderful when you surf with your friends.

Nick was intrigued. "Are you guys surfers?" he asked.

The big man chuckled, side-burns grinned broadly and the quiet man with the hat, shook his head. Michael glanced again at the quiet man. He returned Michael's gaze and nodded his head slightly. A glint of firelight sparkled from his darkly shaded eyes as an invisible plasma charge arced across the campfire and into Michael's forehead. Michael's head recoiled backward imperceptibly as the psychic connection was completed. In a single heartbeat, millions of alien emotions, images and ideas channeled through Michael's mind and into his subconscious. For reasons known only to himself, the quiet man with the hat had chosen Michael to carry this secret transcription. Michael was the chosen vessel. He would be the conductor, the guide, on an adventure that would fulfill a destiny yet unknown. Michael's head drooped momentarily. He looked deep into the yellow heart of the fire as his mind gradually regenerated and began to register the sounds of the lively campfire discussion once again.

The men's conversation wandered from the joys of surfing to the wonder of the camaraderie that true surfers share. They began to relate vivid descriptions of their favorite surfing spots. When surfers gather together, it's always the same.

"Should we tell these guys about the secret spot?" asked the big man. They all nodded.

He began to describe an uncrowded point break where he and his friends surfed.

"It takes any swell direction and has perfect little peelers. It's not far from here, located about forty miles south of..."

"Kaboooom! Yahaaa...eecek"

A loud explosion, screams and teenage laughter interrupted the man's story. Suddenly the area was filled with the commotion typically associated with a boisterous beach party well under way.

Nick and Michael jumped up and looked in the direction of the explosion. What they beheld was incredible. A mushroom cloud billowed skyward from a roaring camp fire. Someone had tossed a cherry bomb into the beach fire causing the explosion. The strange mist had vanished and was replaced by the smoke of a dozen beach fires. Over a hundred clamorous teenagers littered the beach. Nick gazed at Michael with wide-eyed amazement.

"Where the hell did all this come from?" he shrieked. His eyes continued darting about nervously. Michael was silent. A strange expression had fallen across his face. He tapped Nick on the shoulder.

"Look!" yelled Michael.

"They're gone!" blurted Nick as he looked back toward their fire.

"That's right," said Michael, feeling an icy shiver run down his spine. "But the question is, where did they go?"

They stood motionless and stupefied, staring about in disbelief. Soon the sound of a familiar voice rang out.

"Hey, Michael, Nick! Come join us! Where in the hell have you guys been?"

Nick and Michael stood paralyzed. They felt detached from reality.

AJ ran across the beach to his friends. "I thought you blokes would never get here!" he said.

He studied his friend's faces.

"Mates...are you okay? Why are you standing by this old smokin' campfire?" he asked incredulously. AJ studied their queer behavior. "C'mon over to our fire...the girls are here!" he yelled. He slapped Nick on the shoulder.

Michael and Nick finally noticed AJ, but still alternated between looking at each other and the burned-out campfire at their feet. AJ grabbed Michael by the shoulders and shook him.

"Hey...are we having an attack of the zombies here, or haven't you guys seen a beach party before?"

AJ's comment finally broke their spell. Nick began to laugh uneasily. AJ grinned at Michael.

"Hey, ya ole bloke, guess who's been here waiting patiently for you to arrive?"

"Is Monica here?" asked Michael excitedly. He quickly recovered and focused his attention on AJ. AJ nodded his head vigorously as he began leading them away from their fire. As they plodded across the squeaky white sand, Nick tugged on AJ's sleeve and looked into his eyes.

"Did you..." Nick stammered "...did you see what happened to those three guys who were standing by our camp fire?"

AJ gave Nick a quizzical smile. "What guys, mate?" he replied, smiling weirdly. "Hey, me little Italian Guinea...you okay?" he joked. His head cocked sideways like the RCA dog.

AJ's response angered Michael.

"What do you mean, what guys!" he said, glaring back. "You know...you remember," stammered Michael.

Michael began rubbing the back of his neck. Nick interrupted their conversation.

"Yeah, they were the same three guys that were sitting next to us in the restaurant this morning."

AJ studied his friend's faces carefully. He was hoping to see some sign that they were playing a practical joke on him. Soon he realized that they were not kidding.

"Jeez, I'm sorry, mates...no, I didn't see anybody," he said uneasily. "I didn't even see you two until a few minutes ago."

Nick and Michael stopped dead and looked at each other. Nick finally spoke up.

"This is weird and...I don't like it! We were sitting with them," said Nick. "We drank their beer...and they were telling us surf stories...right?" His eyes began darting about. "Am I crazy?" he blurted. "Are we both crazy?"

"Relax," said AJ with a grin, "she'll be right, mates." This was one of the Australian slang phrases that neither Nick or Michael understood. They would always look at each other and grin when ever AJ used it.

"Oh, hell," replied Michael, "lets worry about it later. Right now...the girls!"

Two young girls approached from the campfire. Michael immediately recognized one of them. It was Monica!

"Is everything okay, AJ?" asked one of the girls.

"No worries me little Sheilas," replied AJ (another bit of Australian slang). "Just a little man talk here."

"Hi Monica!" piped Michael to the attractive, sandy-blond haired girl. "Wow...it's really bitchen seeing you again. You're looking great!"

Monica displayed perfect, gleaming teeth.

"It's good to see you too, Michael. I was beginning to think that you weren't coming."

She turned to the girl standing beside her.

"Oh, Michael, Nick, this is my friend, Andi Randell. She and her mother are visiting from Los Angeles."

Andi smiled as she allowed her eyes to linger on Nick. Her smile grew wider.

"I've heard so much about you, Nick," said Andi.

Nick chuckled nervously.

"Hope it all was good," he quipped.

"Oh yes," she said. Her blue eyes caught the firelight. "It's all good," she confirmed.

Nick began to blush

AJ observed the various exchanges. He sighed and pulled out a red and white, crush proof cigarette package from his T-shirt pocket.

"Marlboro," he thought. "Crazy names these yanks come up with for their bloody weeds."

He flipped open the box, pulled out a fresh cigarette and lit it up. He drew the first big drag, sucking it deeply into his lungs. He held his breath momentarily, allowing the nicotine to absorb into the walls of his lungs.

"First drag's always the sweetest," he thought. "But some day I've gotta give up these bloody things."

"Monica says you're a hot surfer," said Andi, her gaze still locked on Nick.

AJ chuckled at her remark, "Yeah, he's hot, until he falls off that barge of his!"

They all laughed.

"It's better than standing backwards on a toothpick and wagging your butt!" replied Nick.

They laughed again. Monica leaned forward in an exaggerated belly laugh. When she bent over, Michael reached across and flicked at the cigarette in AJ's mouth. The tip of the cigarette exploded throwing sparks all over the place. AJ yelped as a spark landed on his nose. He spat the extinguished cigarette into the cool sand.

He gave Michael a menacing look.

"Damn you, Mike, you bastard," he blurted.

Michael chuckled as he slid his arm back around Monica's slim waist. He heard some scrabbling and leaned back to have a look. AJ was kneeling in the cool sand, searching for his cigarette and complaining into the darkness.

Michael and Monica were making up for lost time, and before long they had entwined in a close embrace next to the fire. AJ and Nick had begun a game of beach football, utilizing a knotted-up towel. They took turns running for passes thrown by Andi. The game escalated and soon they were chasing each other between the campfires. The rules were simple. Whoever happened to be carrying the towel was fair game.

By midnight, most of the beach party had scattered and the campfires were reduced to glowing embers. Michael and Monica were still entangled and Nick and Andi sat side-by-side near the fire's edge. AJ lay on his back, with his head resting on the towel-football, apparently asleep. Suddenly, Nick spoke up.

"What do you think really happened, Michael?" he asked. "I mean, do you think we could have been dreaming or hallucinating or something?"

Michael did not reply as he unwrapped himself from Monica and pushed up on one elbow. He grabbed a stick from the fire and began poking at the yellow embers. Tiny sparks drifted into the night sky. He watched them rise until they disappeared.

"They were there, Michael," continued Nick. "We drank their beer!" He burped slightly for emphasis. Michael continued to stare into the fire.

"I believe they were here tonight for a reason, just like at the restaurant." Nick paused again. "They may even be here right now."

Andi and Monica looked at each other, confused over the one-sided conversation. Then AJ lifted his head. He glanced around at the deserted, smoldering campfires.

"Are you sure it was the same guys from the restaurant?" he asked nervously.

Monica could not contain her curiosity any longer.

"What are you guys talking about?" she begged.

No one answered, so she gripped Michael's chin and twisted his face toward hers. She cocked her head slightly and asked again. "What are they talking about?"

"Heee, heee, haaa...there's a maniac on the loose!" said Michael, giving his best Boris Karloff imitation. He's escaped from an asylum...yeah...on the east coast! Yeah...heh, heh, heh!" He rubbed his hands together menacingly. "And now, he's on the loose...and he's looking for young beautiful, teen-aged victims!"

FAMILY VALUES

The morning sunlight streamed into the small kitchen through the window above the sink. It filtered its way through the fragrant steam of freshly made coffee, bacon and eggs and created sunny splotches of light on the well-worn oak flooring. Nick sat at the small solid maple kitchen table, eating the breakfast his mother had prepared. He chewed thoughtfully as he leafed through a family photo album. Outside, the clear morning air was crisp and uncommonly cool for mid-August. He heard the sound of a car approaching.

Michael piloted his Plymouth Barracuda skillfully around the horseshoe shaped driveway. The car's wide, low-profile tires squeaked on the polished cement surface as he cranked the steering wheel to the left and parked. The driveway lay between the meticulously groomed lawn and enclosed front porch of the small, three bedroom ranch-style home. He switched off the key and the dependable 273 Commando V8 motor chugged to a halt. As he strolled up to the familiar front door of the Giovani residence, he smelled an inviting mixture of scents coming through the open living room window. He stepped up and knocked on the door.

In moments a petite woman with medium length chestnut colored hair appeared and greeted Michael.

"Good morning Mikey!" she said cheerfully.

Michael grinned unabashedly. Normally he preferred being called Michael or Mike, but his best friend's mother named him Mikey and he enjoyed hearing it from her.

"Good morning Mrs. Giovani," said Michael, his voice dripping with charm. "How are you on this beautiful morning?"

Mrs. Giovani hurried back to the kitchen. As Michael crossed the living room, Nick called out from the kitchen.

"Mike...you're early!"

Michael entered the cheery kitchen and inhaled deeply through his nose.

"It smells like heaven in here, Mrs. Giovani," said Michael, continuing to drip.

She turned from the stove and looked over her reading glasses at the young man standing in the doorway. She smiled sweetly.

"There's plenty, Michael, please...sit down." She motioned with her spatula to the kitchen table. Michael smiled sheepishly as he walked around the large wooden table. He slid out one of the low-back western style chairs and sat down directly across from Nick. Nick glanced up from the album.

"I was just looking at some pictures of my dad," said Nick. He paused as his eyes met his mother's. She smiled sadly.

"Joseph would have been 49 today," replied Mrs. Giovani. "Today is his birthday." She approached the boys.

"How is your family, Mikey?" She placed a cup in front of him and filled it with steaming, black coffee from a glazed-porcelain coffee pot.

"They're all fine," said Michael as he sipped the fragrant black liquid from the thick clay mug. Mrs. Giovani scurried back to the stove.

"My mom is visiting with her sister and my dad and his girlfriend are out of town till next week," said Michael absently.

Mrs. Giovani approached Michael again. She leaned forward and placed a fully loaded plate in front of him. The big oval platter clinked heavily against the solid wood surface of the table. Steam rose up from heaps of eggs, fried potatoes, ham and buttered sourdough toast. Then she placed a napkin on the table and laid a knife, fork and spoon on it. Michael required no further persuasion as he dove hungrily into the food. He shoveled scrambled eggs into his mouth with one hand while simultaneously dumping catsup on the potatoes with the other.

"Nicky, eat your breakfast," begged Mrs. Giovani as she watched Michael stuff his cheeks full. Nick looked at his mother with a *give me a break...I'm not your little Nicky any more* expression. He went back to the album. Mrs. Giovani shook her head and sucked air through her front teeth disdainfully. Her slippers made scuffing noises as she left the room. Michael watched her exit.

"I've been kinda' thinking about that incident at the beach party last night. Did you tell your mom?" asked Michael.

Nick chewed pensively. Finally he replied.

"I don't know...I guess I'm concerned that it might upset her or something. Its just been so weird. Maybe someone's just playing a gag on us or something."

Just then Mrs. Giovani returned to the kitchen and went to the sink.

"What time are you going to be home, Nicky?" she asked. She began to rinse the breakfast dishes.

"I don't know, mom. Maybe around four o'clock or so...right, Mike?"

"Yeah, Mrs. Giovani, about four," replied Michael without looking up.

She turned off the water, then dried her hands on her apron. She turned first to Nick, then Michael with a pained expression.

"Well, what are you two going to do about lunch?" she asked.

Michael eased back into the low-back chair and patted his stomach.

"After this breakfast we won't need lunch, Mrs. Giovani. In fact I may not eat again till tomorrow!"

Michael looked at the album in front of Nick. Suddenly, his face lit up. "Hey...I've got a great idea! Come on, Buddy," he said to Nick. He stood. "Thanks for the great breakfast Mrs. Giovani."

"Oh...you're welcome, honey," she replied.

She kissed them both on the cheek as was customary. She had always accepted Michael as her second son. The boys turned and walked toward the front door.

Nick pumped Michael as they left, "Where are we going, Mike?"

"I'll tell you later," replied Michael, "right now we have to go get AJ." He hurried out the front door.

It was nearly noon before Michael, Nick and AJ arrived at the Green Field Family Cemetery. They had picked up AJ and made several other stops along the way. Michael parked the car at the base of a long sloping grass knoll. He got out, went to the rear of the car and took a brown paper grocery bag from the trunk of the car. The wind was cool and gusting from the west.

Green Field Cemetery was huge, covering over four square miles. An amazing 2,700 acres of carefully groomed lawn accented with endless rows of tidy, analogous grave markers. Nick headed off in the general direction of his Dad's grave.

After about forty minutes of continual searching, Michael was beginning to feel a bit frustrated and impatient.

"What a kook! How could he forget the location of his own fathers grave marker?" thought Michael incredulously.

"Wasn't it over there, Nick?" asked Michael, pointing to his right. "Last time we were here I remember heading that way."

Nick held his Da Bull cap on his head with his right hand as he squinted into the wind.

"I think when we came in we should have turned right," said Nick. He moved his right hand to gesture in that direction. At that moment a gust of wind descended and swirled around him like a vortex. His cap was lifted up and away. Nick watched it spin clockwise as it rose skyward, riding the gust like a balloon. He raced after the cap, but each time he was close to capturing it, the wind scooped it up again.

Two years before Nick had attended a Greg Noll book signing at the Santa Lina Surf Shop. He bought the hat then and Greg Noll had autographed the bill for him. Nick cherished that hat and had worn it every day since.

Finally, a particularly strong burst lifted it thirty feet and released it. It flipped about as it fell to earth about one hundred yards to the southeast. Nick bolted after it. At the last second he dove through the air and pounced. He lay momentarily on the grass panting, then rolled over and lifted the cap triumphantly. Gradually his eyes focused beyond the cap and his mouth fell agape in amazement. There, just two yards away sat a small gray Italian marble marker that read, *In memory of Joseph Patrick Giovani, a great husband, father and waterman. August 17, 1946 to June 24, 1995.*

Michael now approached and observed his friend lying supine and apparently paralyzed. Michael, however, also began to gape in disbelief at the small headstone.

"You found it, Nick!" he exclaimed.

AJ joined them.

"Yeh found yer dad's grave, mate?" he asked clumsily.

"Yeah, AJ...sshhh!" said Michael.

They stood above Nick for long moments, staring quietly down. Finally, Michael hunkered down, Indian style and reached into the big shopping bag. He produced an unopened gallon of Almaden red wine.

"I know it's kind of early to drink, but Nick and I felt that it would be appropriate to drink a toast to his Dad on his birthday," said Michael. He cracked the seal and handed the bottle to Nick.

"Happy birthday, Dad," said Nick as he raised it to his lips and gulped loudly.

Nick handed the jug back to Michael, who glanced toward the sky.

"This one's for you, Mr. Giovani." Michael raised the bottle and took a long drink.

The jug was passed to AJ.

"Hope you 're catching some eight foot clouds up there!" said AJ with a little laugh. Then he continued softly. "Happy birthday, mate." AJ sat.

Once again, Michael reached into the bag and withdrew another smaller jar filled with clear liquid. He smiled proudly.

"We brought a little Pacific from your old spot, Mr. Giovani...Wild Hook!"

He handed the jar to Nick who unscrewed the lid, leaned forward over the grave and ceremoniously poured the sea water into the grass near the small headstone.

"We all knew how much you liked to surf there, so this is kind of a birthday present." Nick paused. His voice cracked.

"Happy Birthday...Dad," he choked.

Nick looked at his friends. His eyes welled with tears.

"Thanks guys. I know that somewhere...he's watching."

AJ attempted to soften the edge on Michael's sorrow.

"You know mate, it's just not right. He should be out there surfing with us."

"He is...he's always with us," confirmed Nick.

The wind blew Nick's curly hair as he rolled over on the soft grass. He stretched his arms back and cradled his head in his hands. AJ took another drink from the jug and wiped his mouth.

"Yeah, I think he is too," confirmed Michael, "especially when I see you surf, Nicky. Your style is a lot like your dad's."

AJ handed Nick the jug. He took a swig and rolled over on his side, resting his head on his right hand.

"Remember that day in the winter of eighty-one," said Nick, pausing with his eyes turned slightly upward. He shifted his gaze to Michael.

"Remember when Dad and Richie Todd were the only ones out at Steamer's Lane."

"Remember it!" said Michael. "It seems like yesterday. It was a cold gray winter day. A big northwest swell had been pounding California for three days. Finally it settled down enough to be rideable and your dad talked Richie into paddling out. It kept getting bigger with each wave...then sets were starting to form on 3rd reef...almost a mile out!"

Michael looked at AJ.

"Nick and I were just kids. God, your Dad caught that one wave...must have been over twenty feet! Man, I was scared, but excited at the same time."

"Talk about scared," said Nick. He shivered slightly. "I had nightmares about that day for a long time afterwards."

Michael continued.

"Then he paddled into another wave out on third reef. When he dropped in, it just heaved up and closed over him. He got stuck in the pit, lost his board and was pounded for a good 15 minutes...non-stop! Man, my heart was doing flips! When I looked over at Nick...his face was as white as a ghost!"

Nick stared vacantly at Michael. His mind went back to the day. He recalled how he had raced up to his father after the long swim in. He remembered standing there, hugging his dad's waist with all his strength and whispering to himself, "Thank you God!"

AJ pulled the wine jug from Nick's grip.

"Hey, Nicky, remember that story your dad told us about the surfing safari they took? When they got a fix-it ticket in Santa Barbara for loud tail pipes? And the BA they hung at the bus full of girls?"

"Uh-huh," replied Nick, recovering from his reverie and brightening slightly. "Yeah...my dad got a fix-it ticket on his old Desoto for loud pipes. He didn't want to have an out-of-town ticket hanging over his head, so he decided to try and get it signed off while they were still in town. The old car had a 331 cubic inch Chrysler Hemi-head engine that drove a dual Smitty flow-thru exhaust system. It created quite a roar, especially during start and stop driving through town. They decided to use some surfer ingenuity to achieve a quick fix. They muffled the dual pipes temporarily by stuffing steel wool into the Smitty's with a long pole. The results were impressive. The old coach's interior became so quiet that they could actually converse in normal tones! Feeling confident, they began cruising around Ventura looking for a CHP officer. They spotted two black and white motorcycles outside the Jolly Tiger restaurant on Chapala Street. When the cops came out, my dad explained the situation to them and they agreed to check out the repairs. One of the officers stationed himself behind the tail pipes, while the other directed my dad's brother, Dave, to rev it up. Dave revved the engine slightly.

"No, kid!" ordered the officer, "I said, rev it up!" Dave looked in the rear view mirror at my dad, who stood next to the CHP. Dave shrugged his shoulders.

"He mashed the accelerator to the floor. The Rochester four-barrel carburetor opened up and the Hemi exploded into full power. A rush of unencumbered exhaust blasted through the tuned pipes, loosening miles of unburned carbon dust. Huge clouds of dirty black smoke blasted out the tail pipes – the officer and my dad jumped back in alarm (the old Desoto was a real sleeper and my dad liked it that way). Like miniature artillery shells, the small gray steel-wool balls came firing out and ricocheted off the spit-polished toes of the CHP officers knee-high boots. Needless to say...my dad didn't get *that* ticket signed off."

The boys began to laugh aloud as the effects of the story combined with the wine. Their mood had transformed from solemn to giddy.

Michael slammed his fist into the ground and chortled uncontrollably. He continued. "Yeah...and that was the same trip that they were cruising down Coast Highway on their way back to Santa Lina and Dave and their Hawaiian friend Glenn Lee decided to hang a BA at what he believed was a tourist bus. They heard shrill screams coming from the bus' interior. It turned out to be full of girls from a Seventh-day Adventist summer camp!"

"Yeah...about seven miles later the same bus pulled up along side them at a gas station in San Simeon," screamed Michael. "Glenn yanked down his baggies, opened the front door and prepared to hang another BA. My dad grabbed his baggies and pushed him out the passenger side of the car. The baggies came off and Glenn went reeling across the gas station driveway, bare naked. Dad pulled the door shut and locked it as the girls began screaming. Glenn panicked and ran around the old Desoto looking for a way in. My dad grinned hideously as he started the Desoto and began to pull away very slowly. Glenn ran after them and leaped onto the rear of the car. He sprawled across the trunk lid with his bare feet balanced on the oversized chrome bumper. His nose and lips were smeared against the rear window as he stared with horror into the car's interior. Dad continued cruising down the main boulevard, honking his horn, for three blocks before he pulled over and let Glenn back inside."

"Man, they sure knew how to have fun," whooped Michael.

"They used to take surfing safaris all the time," said Michael. He looked at Nick, and AJ.

"What do you say, guys? Want to do a little traveling?" Michael continued. "We're meeting with the girls tomorrow morning. We could see if they want to go with us! Come on you guys...let's make some memories of our own."

There was no response. Michael sighed, turned over on his back and folded his arms across his chest.

After a long pause, AJ spoke up. "You know Nick, your dad really lived. I mean the things he did, the places he went, the great surf he surfed." AJ choked up slightly.

"His memories live on, in you, Nick, and you, Michael." AJ rolled over on his back too. He stared thoughtfully up at the blue sky.

"Yeah, that's the way I want my life to be," said Nick, in a subdued pensive tone. "Maybe a surfin' safari would be fun," he thought. "You're right Mike," announced Nick, "we should make some memories of our own!"

NEXT MORNING...5:30 AM

"Tap...tuppa, tuppa, tap, tap..."

Nick drummed his fingers nervously against the oversized truck steering wheel. His right hand tapped a base beat and his left was the snare as his favorite rock tune ricocheted around in his head. He cleared his throat to rid it of early morning phlegm.

"Did you tell the girls when to be ready?" he asked.

"Yep," replied Michael, "I told them that we'd be outside Monica's house waiting at five-thirty sharp...so let's keep it quiet, 'cause I don't think it would be cool to wake her parents."

Nick raised his wrist to his face. He depressed the top button on his Casio G-Shock Chrono. The LED lit up the digital face. It read five-thirty AM.

"Andi says Monica's mom is cool," said Nick, "maybe I should honk just once."

"Yeah, sure, dolt...how cool would you be if you got woke up at five in the morning?" quipped Michael.

"Yeah, maybe you have a point there," said Nick, reflecting, "I guess there's no one quite like my mom."

At that moment the front porch light came on and Monica and Andi came rushing out the big double door. They scarcely noticed the boys as they lowered backpacks and sleeping bags on the front steps and bustled busily across the side lawn. They made their way steadily around the south side of the house and disappeared through a wooden gate. A few minutes later the gate opened and Michael could see the nose of a white surfboard emerging. He and Nick jumped out of the truck and hurried across the wet lawn to assist them. They grabbed the surfboards while the girls returned to the front porch to retrieve their surfing gear.

A moment later they were packing all the gear into the rear of Nick's truck. Michael watched Monica adjust the surfboards so her board would fit neatly. As she leaned over, her long golden hair fell forward across her face. She flipped it back over her shoulder in a quick tossing movement. It made a snapping noise, like a bundle of hundreds of tiny flaxen lashes. Michael became momentarily hypnotized by her incredible natural beauty. He felt himself being attracted. She turned to face him and their eyes met briefly. Like magic, they continued to be drawn closer. Finally, their lips met and for long moments they embraced each other.

Nick was busily re-adjusting the gear around the surfboards. He moved over to help AJ. They looked at each other and smiled.

Michael, was unaware of his audience. He whispered into Monica's ear. "I'm glad you were ready. I couldn't wait to see you."

"You said be ready by five-thirty," said Monica.

Michael hugged her tighter.

"You feel good," he said, kissing her once more.

Nick was becoming impatient. He spoke up. "Heh...uh, look, why don't you guys just stay here and you can catch up with us later?"

Michael looked at his two friends. They both displayed roguish grins.

"You ought to try this before breakfast," replied Michael, "its the only way to start the day."

With that, Monica pulled him closely once again and kissed him.

Nick turned to Andi who stood by his side. He pinched her cheek softly.

"What do you say. Is it worth a try?" She moved close and he kissed her.

"Okay, okay, enough of this," said Nick, pulling free of Andi. He moved toward the driver's side of the truck. "We've got waves to catch!" he ordered.

They all laughed as Nick opened the door and pulled himself up and behind the wheel of the big Chevy. AJ ran to the front passenger door and opened it.

"Shotgun!" yelled Michael, as he whooshed up behind AJ and forced him into the truck. AJ was trapped between Nick and Michael on the big bench seat.

Monica shook her head and giggled at the boys' antics. She and Andi walked across the lawn to the driveway. They hopped inside Monica's 1989 Volvo.

The waves at Seacliff Beach were small and mushy and the south wind blew steadily onshore. Michael sat, hugging his knees and staring drearily down at the sand.

"We rushed our ass off for this slop," he mumbled to himself.

Nick could tell that Michael was upset by the conditions.

"You want to check the beaches?" he asked in an attempt to cheer Michael. It did not work. Michael began to smooth the white sand with his hand.

"Let's just go," Michael said suddenly. "Man...I'd really like to get away from Santa Lina." He paused momentarily. "You know, I think I might know where that spot is. The one those strange dudes were talking about."

Nick laughed nervously.

"I didn't think that you were even concerned about those guys, Mike. I figured that you've just been ignoring the whole situation. Besides, how could you possibly know. Every time they start explaining how to find the place something happens to interrupt them. They never finish their story."

Michael rested his chin on top of his knees as he stared toward the horizon.

"I don't know," he replied finally, "its just this feeling I got when they were talking. I felt like I could almost see it."

He glanced up at Nick.

"How 'bout it, let's take a little trip south. Whattaya say?"

Nick looked back suspiciously.

"What's so great about down south? It's the same as here. Crowded, smoggy, crappy attitudes."

Monica interrupted their conversation. "Hey guys, maybe we could all camp out on the way? And, AJ, my cousin Lisa wants to meet you. Maybe she'll want to come along too. She's real cute."

A huge grin expanded across AJ's face. He wagged his head up and down in exaggerated concurrence.

Monica winked at Andi.

"That *would* be fun," said Andi, winking back.

"C'mon, Nick," said Michael attempting to re-focus the conversation, "the water's warmer, the sun's hotter..."

"I don't know," said Nick hesitantly.

"Aw, c'mon!" said Michael more vigorously. "Lets do it!"

Nick raised his eyebrows and tossed his head towards the girls. He displayed his little boy smile.

"When do we leave?"

Monica and Andi hugged each other excitedly. Monica shivered slightly, "I'm gonna get my sweatshirt out of the truck." She and Andi began walking toward the truck.

Michael glanced at Nick and AJ.

"AJ, I'll call you later," said Michael, "and we'll meet at Nick's house later tonight to plan the trip. How's that sound?"

AJ grinned expansively. "Sounds good to me!"

It was eight PM when the friends finally gathered at Nick's house. They lay clustered around the fireplace in the Giovani's cozy living room. A small oakwood fire cast silvery reflections over their faces. Nick reclined in his father's favorite chair. His feet were elevated. Michael lay in front of the fire with his head propped on his left arm. He busily jabbed a poker into the burning log. AJ lay on his back on top of the big, overstuffed leather couch.

"You know," said Nick, "I've been thinking about those guys we saw at the cafe and that secret spot. Now, Mike says he thinks he knows where it is."

"Yeah, so what mate," replied AJ, sleepily.

"Well," continued Nick, with a slight catch in his voice, "you know how much my dad loved the ocean and surfing?"

Mike and AJ turned to watch Nick as he continued.

"I told you guys about how he used to tell me surfing stories before I went to sleep, when I was a little kid."

"Yeah, your mom said they were your bedtime stories," replied Michael.

"And Duke Kahanumoku was your bedtime hero," added AJ.

Michael chuckled. "I remember her saying that whenever she tried tell you a real bedtime story, you'd ask when the surfing part would start...or are there be any dolphins...or where are the surfboards."

All three laughed now as Nick reached for his Pepsi. There was a long pause then he took a sip. The fire flared and crackled in the silence. Nick began again.

"Well, I've been thinking and that story those men were telling is almost identical to the one my dad used to tell me when I was a little boy. In fact, I remember begging him re-tell it over and over. The story was about a surfing Shangri-La, where the waves were perfect, the sun always shined and the water was clear, warm and never crowded."

"Sound like a surfers dream, mate," said AJ.

Nick gazed at the picture of his dad that sat on the mantel. In the picture his dad wore a large straw lifeguard hat. He recited a part of the story. "When you walk over that first mound of sand, a feeling of excitement fills your soul. Breaking on the horizon are perfect little peelers. Each wave is unique, individually perfect. The sun shines brightly, giving a magical, soft pastel glow to all the surroundings. Several dolphins leap suddenly from the water as they race to match the pitch on the face of an iridescent wall of water. The waves are all sizes depending upon where you paddle, and the water sparkles like diamonds. Then you see *them* sitting on their boards and they beckon for you to join them. I used to always ask, do you really surf with them Dad? You bet I do, my father would say."

Michael rolled over to his stomach. He crossed his hands and rested his chin on them. The fire warmed his face. AJ still stared up at the ceiling. The firelight flickered and played across Nick's features.

Mrs. Giovani had been standing by the doorway, listening. She wiped a tear from her eye as she quietly turned and walked back to her room.

Michael stirred suddenly and drew in a quick breath. He pushed up to his knees. "I'll bet the spot they were talking about is between San Simeon and Santa Barbara somewhere. A small cove, hidden by the cliffs. Probably takes a southwest swell..."

"Shoot, Michael," said Nick, annoyed, "do you always have to be so damn logical? Don't you have any magic in you? Can't you imagine a bitchen, imaginary place like the one in the story?"

"Sure...in my dreams!" replied Michael, with a laugh. "If there is a secret spot, then it'll be like any other place, only it won't be crowded with Agro's or polluted with a bunch of butt waggers...like him!" He tossed a pillow at AJ.

"Sounds bloody fantastic, mate!" said AJ, jumping up and wiggling his back-side at Michael.

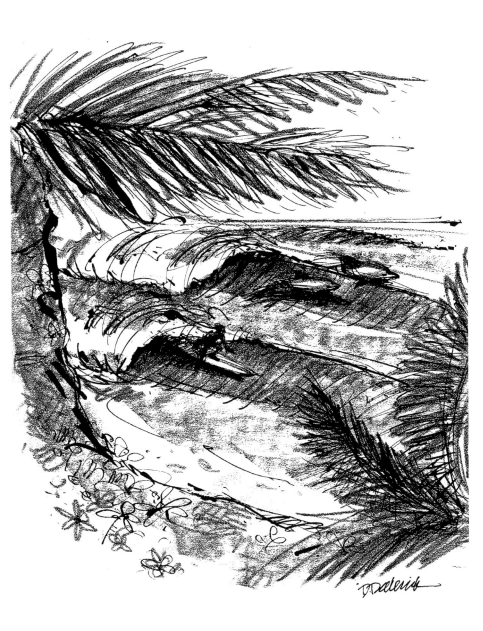

He threw the pillow back. "And speaking of reality," continued AJ, "what about this trip? Are we going or what?"

Michael did not respond. Something familiar about Nick's story was gnawing away at his subconscious. Something he felt an odd affinity with.

"So Nick...who are *They?*" asked Michael, carefully. "Did your dad ever tell you?"

Nick considered the question.

"You know, the weird thing is that my dad never had to tell me. I always felt like I knew. But once he did mention that it was the Duke's spot."

AJ interrupted impatiently. "Look, are we ever gonna talk about this safari, mates?" He scrutinized his friends. His comment was ignored.

"Nick, are you sure you're not mixing up your memories with what those weird guys in the cafe were saying?" asked Michael.

"Heh, Mike, let your imagination go. Let a little magic into your heart," replied Nick.

Michael mumbled to himself, "Magic, hah! I've got some magic...right here."

He reached down and grabbed momentarily at the fly of his 501 Levi's.

Nick laughed and ejected himself from the recliner. He leaped through the air toward Michael, landing with an exaggerated bounce and shaking his hair like he had seen many times on TV wrestling. He and Michael began grappling. They laughed boisterously. AJ leaped from the couch and wedged himself between them.

"C'mon you guys. Let's get this trip figured out!"

"Okay, okay!" barked Michael. "Let's discuss the bloody Aussie's safari."

It was about ten-thirty when Michael finally stood, stretched expansively and yawned.

"I'll see you guys tomorrow afternoon...I've got karate early in the morning."

As Michael headed for the door, AJ stood to leave.

"I'll see you tomorrow, Nick," said AJ, flashing a salute at Nick. "And thanks for the hospitality, matey."

Nick acknowledged his friends, but remained sitting in the big overstuffed recliner. He picked up a carefully framed photograph from the end table next to the chair. It contained a photograph of a man wearing a floppy hat, holding a surfboard, standing next to an old Chevrolet panel truck.

Inside Nick a small voice whispered, "Do you really surf with *them,* Dad?"

MAGIC

The early morning sunshine streamed in through the high windows of the Omi-Kan Karate Dojo. It radiated off the flat white walls and diffused into pale, blue-tinted shadowless illumination. Michael kneeled rigid and straight-backed on the hardwood floor of the small karate studio. He and fifteen other students lined up directly opposite Sensei Omi.

"Sei-shup...machso...reght!" commanded Omi brusquely.

The entire class moved in unison, bowing and placing their hands on the floor in front of them. The thumb and index finger of each hand were joined to form a triangle. Then they continued to bend until each forehead touched the center of the triangle and the hardwood floor. Sensei stood majestically and raised his hands, palm up.

"Up!" he ordered.

Everyone rose and immediately launched into the strenuous warm-up exercises that preceded each class. Michael had been a student of Sensei Omi for over three years and they had become very good friends. Omi seemed to really understand Michael and kept a close eye on him. Today, however, he noticed that Michael's concentration seemed to be a bit off.

After twenty minutes of warm-up, Omi divided the class into individual groups based upon their rankings. A brown belt was assigned to each group to assist the students in practicing the basics of Shoto-kan. Shoto-kan is one of the most ancient forms of Martial Art in existence. In Japanese, it means literally, the trees and the sea. Michael was drawn to Shoto-kan after watching a demonstration at a local adult education exposition. After three trial classes, he enrolled in the school. That was in 1992 and since then he had attained six belt rankings. He was now a third degree brown belt and the next level was first degree black belt. This would be a difficult step, requiring two days of testing in Los Angeles, before a panel of high ranking judges. Michael did not like tests of any kind. They made him nervous, very nervous.

At about one hour into the class Sensei began the sparring practice. Michael enjoyed this because it was a chance for him to apply the technique that he had learned. Sparring was very close to authentic hand-to-hand confrontation. The class formed two lines that rotated from one student to the next. The sparing would last for half an hour, then the class would practice the Katas. The Katas were designed to incorporate the multitude of blocks, punches, kicks, movements and tricks that Sensei taught them. The Kata was a dance that had to be performed perfectly. In fact, learning and executing the Katas properly was the most important task in obtaining upper belt rankings.

Finally Sensei held up his arms and the class activity ceased. He commanded the class to line up and they did so according to rank, white belts being the lowest and brown belts the highest.

"Aaachso...reght!" he commanded.

Again the class kneeled and bowed respectfully. When all students had raised their heads, Omi spoke.

"You must all remember that pure karate is for self-defense only. It must never be used unless you must protect your friends, loved ones or someone in need."

"Hei...Sensei!" replied the class in perfect unison.

He bowed once again and the class returned his bow, then he dismissed them.

When the others had departed, Michael approached Sensei. Omi was mopping his face and neck with a white towel.

"I won't be coming to class next week, Sensei," said Michael. "My friends and I are taking a short trip down south."

Omi watched him carefully.

"Michael-san, I wish to speak with you. Let us please sit," he urged.

They both moved to the corner of the room and sat cross-legged on the floor.

"I have noticed in the past few classes that your concentration is off. You don't seem to have your normal balance and timing. It's as if your heart and mind are not in your karate." Omi's eyes studied Michael's face carefully. "Is anything wrong, Michael-san?"

Michael felt awkward. He paused momentarily.

"I...I don't know, Sensei," he stumbled, "I guess I'm frustrated or something." Michael was unable to hide the dejected expression on his face.

"Would you like to tell me what is frustrating you, Michael-san?"

Michael matched Omi's steady gaze. Omi nodded with encouragement as he explained.

"I've been here for 3 years, Sensei, and I'm still a brown belt. I don't seem to be getting anywhere. I'll never get my black belt!" He paused, then began again. "It feels as if I'm stuck where I am and can't go any further."

There was another long pause. Omi nodded for Michael to continue.

"I feel as if I might disgrace you."

Omi continued to nod his head, reassuringly until Michael had finished. Then Omi spoke.

"Michael, you are doing well...sometimes one can lose one's center. When that happens, concentration is lost." Sensei paused, his dark eyes piercing. "Michael-san, you are always searching here, there and everywhere, but..."

Omi burrowed his index forcefully into Michael's chest.

"...Not in the right place." He paused again. "When you realize this, that is when you will get *unstuck* and be able to progress to the next level."

He considered the wisdom of his teacher's words as he stared into Omi's coal black eyes.

"Yes, Sensei, you are probably right. But what you say is easier said, than done."

Omi smiled warmly and stood.

"Ah...Michael-san, you'd be surprised. When you accept this," he winked at Michael, "all the world becomes magical."

Omi stood and walked toward his office. As he reached the edge of the mat he turned and bowed toward Michael. Then entered his office and closed the door. After a moment Michael stood. He felt slightly shaken by his teacher's little speech.

"How could he know," he spat angrily into his chest. "Again with the damn *magic!*"

While Michael was in karate, Nick was enjoying a dawn patrol at the Wild Hook. He often paddled out alone, especially when he needed to think. Surfing was the perfect elixir when something troubled him. The solitude, combined with the exercise and spiritual imbibe would get him through even the most troubling personal problems.

He had caught a few waves and was taking a slight break. He sat outside the main break and stared out to sea, thinking. Behind him, about twenty yards on the inside reef, were a small cluster of young surfers. Within the group were two young hoodlums with shaved heads, tattoos and matching attitudes. This seemed to be the standard uniform for punk surfers. All morning long the two had intentionally dropped in on Nick and anyone else who had tried to catch a wave. After each ride they grunted obnoxiously and made rude comments to all outside their closed group. It was clear that their behavior was ruining everyone's fun and a beautiful sunny morning. This angered Nick.

Nick had reached the end of his quiet reverie and had decided to catch the next rideable wave and go in.

Suddenly he was visited by a memory from his childhood. He was nine years old and he and his Dad were sitting on their surfboards at 38th Avenue. An obnoxious kid was cutting everybody off, including Nick and his Dad.

"Nicky...look at that guy!" His dad sat with his arms crossed across his chest. "He's miserable! Surfing should be fun! He's definitely not having any fun."

"I'm getting tired of him, Dad!" said Nick. "One more time and I'm gonna run him over!"

Joe responded calmly. "If you do, son...will it make anything better?" He paused and looked into his son's eyes. "It'll only bring you down to his level...you won't be any better than him and you'll be miserable too. Remember, Nicky, if you're courteous and treat people the way you would like to be treated, the reward will be tenfold."

Nick shook his head and cleared away the day-dream. He turned toward the horizon and spotted a nice wave heading his way. Instinctively, he turned his longboard and began to paddle toward the shallow spot on the reef. Out of the corner of his eye he caught the movement of one of the shave-head kids paddling his way. In moments the kid positioned himself directly beneath Nick.

He was going for the wave, a wave that was clearly Nick's. At the last moment Nick stopped paddling and pulled his board up and out of the wave. Instead of getting upset or yelling, he smiled and motioned for the kid to go for it. He even hooted him on encouragingly. The kid flashed past Nick and rode the wave all the way in.

Later that morning Nick loaded his surfboard onto rear of the Suburban. He pulled on his Da Bull surf trunks, then turned to have a last look at the waves. He pondered deeply about what adventures he and his friends might experience on their safari down south. He also wondered if there would be any waves, or if it would be crowded, blown-out or crappy. He felt a mix of excitement and apprehension. As he opened the truck door and prepared to slide into the front seat, the two shave-head surfers walked past his truck. He could overhear their conversation. He stood by the opened door and listened.

"I hate longboarders," said one of the boys. "They think they own the ocean!" The other surfer, the one that Nick had been polite to, did not reply. He just flashed an amiable smile toward Nick. Nick recognized him, smiled back and returned a friendly nod.

Nick inhaled deeply through his nose, then allowed his breath to escape slowly from his lips. The air smelled sweet and the sun was warm upon his bare chest. Nick watched the young shortboarders until they disappeared behind the sandy knoll just before the highway. Once again he heard his father's voice.

"The reward is tenfold."

High Spirits

Michael's stomach bubbled with happy anticipation as he cruised south on spectacular Highway 1. Once past Santa Lina, Highway 1 became a narrow two lane road that cut a hundred mile long serpentine path next to the sheer cliffs and the breathtakingly beautiful northern Pacific ocean. It is a much slower ride south than Highway 101.

The boys cruised along, admiring how the sun drooped lazily over the gray-blue surface of the ocean. It looked as if a brilliant sunset would be in store for them.

"Man, we've been driving for hours," complained Michael. "I need some coffee! Hey, Nick, are you sure the girls will be there when we arrive?"

"Yeah...they said they would leave early so they could nab us a choice camping spot," replied Nick. "And so they wouldn't have to drive Highway 1 in the dark."

Nick yawned expansively. "I could use some coffee too. Let's stop at the next coffee shop."

Michael peered into the rear view mirror. "I wish I could sleep like that AJ," he mused.

"Let's keep watching the road," replied Nick. "We need to find a place where we can get that coffee."

Michael turned to Nick and winked mischievously. "It's sure gonna be nice tonight!"

"Yeah...it is," said Nick with a smile.

Suddenly Nick jerked his head back toward the road. "Look out!" he screamed.

Michael's view of the road was instantly eclipsed by a blurry form. A huge buck had bolted from behind the thick brush that lined the edge of the road. The enormous creature danced madly as its delicate hooves fought to gain traction on the unyielding asphalt. Michael's sharp reflexes gave the buck a split second to clear the front bumper as he hit the brakes and swerved the car to the left. They began to broadslide now, toward the thick brush where the deer had emerged from.

"Lucky deer," thought Michael with unusual calmness. Time seemed to slow down and become strobe-like as the car continued careening sideways at over fifty miles-per-hour.

He steered into the skid and the car corrected instantly as the high performance tires gripped the rough pavement. Immediately, the vehicle slung back around a full 180 degrees and began to cross the road. They were now on a deadly trajectory that would take them off the edge of the pavement and over the sheer cliff. The tires squealed hideously as they left the road and bounced onto the dirt apron. A wall of loose earth fanned up on the driver's side as Michael stomped hard on the brakes. The old Plymouth continued around another ninety degrees. They were now traveling at about thirty-five miles-per-hour; in reverse! Michael craned his head around backwards and stared through the large rear fastback window. He gazed past AJ's terrified face and observed a low earth embankment approaching. It was the kind that highway crews create along the edge of mountain roads to keep carelessly parked cars from rolling away to their oblivion. Beyond the embankment lay a one-thousand feet vertical drop to the chiseled, cobalt blue ocean below.

When the car struck the embankment the tremendous kinetic energy of the slide bulldozed huge hunks of earth over the edge. The dirt bank had stopped them, but the rear of the car slid over the mound to a point on the cars frame just under the drivers seat. They now rested precariously with the rear end hanging over the cliff and the tires spinning in mid-air.

The three sat bolt upright, scared and shaken but unhurt. Huge choking clouds of dust swirled around the cab of the car. The sun was still just above the horizon, but the car's interior was nearly dark as the thick dust obscured most of the remaining sunlight. Michael gripped the steering wheel. His normally large knuckles now stood out bone-white and surreal. He stared straight ahead. Nick gripped the plastic and metal dashboard and AJ gripped the back of Nick's bucket seat.

The classic two-door Plymouth sports coupe had been in Michael's family since his father purchased it from the Chrysler-Plymouth-Dodge showroom floor in 1964. He passed it on to Michael upon the completion of his sophomore year in high school. The Plymouth's husky under-frame now sat balanced on the cliff's edge, rocking like a bizarre teeter-totter.

When the car began sliding, AJ had been rudely awakened. "What happened, mates?" he asked, staring glaze-eyed over the seat. "Are we still alive?"

Michael swallowed hard. "Everyone okay?" He scanned his friends' faces. They both nodded in the affirmative.

"Now, what the hell is that?" exclaimed AJ as he pointed through the front window of the car.

They stared ahead, toward the road, as the golden light of the sunset illuminated an eerie sight. They watched as a strange pulsating haze spilled down from the steep hillside above. It slithered quickly across the road, then rolling like a wave it quickly engulfed them.

"That crap really looks weird!" said Michael, squinting through the windshield.

"Yeah...let's get going, that stuff gives me the creeps," insisted Nick.

Michael re-started the engine and slid the Hurst *Mystery Shifter* four-speed linkage into low gear. He gave it the gas, but the car did not budge. He gunned it again. Still nothing.

"Great!" yelled Michael, "what else is going to happen?"

He glanced over at Nick. "Take a look at what's holding us up out there, would-ja, bud?"

Nick complained as he rolled down the passenger side window and extended his head outside.

"I can't see anything through all this crappy fog," he complained."

He opened the car door and stepped out.

"Yaaahhh!

Nick gripped car door as it swung into the foggy unknown. He was experiencing the terrifying, though familiar sensations of a frequent nightmare he had where he was free-falling, all the while hoping that it was only a dream that he would soon awaken from. This, however, was no dream! He clung with his right arm locked around the opened door, dangling above nothing but the chilly fog-filled air. The door began to swing back and forth in response to his convulsive bodily movements. The coupe began to rock on it's frame

"Oh shit!" he screamed. "Help me, you guys!"

Nick peered down through the fog that poured over the sheer cliff's edge. He gazed past his dangling legs and beyond to the dimly lit ocean and rocks a thousand feet below. He screamed hysterically.

"You guys! It's a straight drop down to the rocks!"

He tightened his grip on the window frame and wrapped his legs around the door as it continued to swing on it's hinges. Rocks and earth began to pour over the edge of the cliff. They all began screaming in unison.

"Yaahhh!"

"Damn it, Nick!" yelled Michael. "Don't move or we'll all go over!"

"Shit," replied Nick, in panic, "do something...my arm is giving out!"

"Maybe I can reach him!" screamed AJ from the back seat. He began to carefully climb forward, but as he moved the car began to rock again. He froze.

"Damn it, AJ!" screamed Michael. "No one move!"

Nick peered down again but diminished light and the fog now obscured the horrific scene below him.

"What are we supposed to do? Stay like this until the whole car slides over?" screamed Nick hoarsely.

"Stay calm!" ordered Michael, "Somebody is bound to drive by." As he peered out the front window he felt a cold, oily sensation jolt through his veins. "But if this fog gets any thicker, they won't see us," he thought in terror.

Suddenly, Michael cocked his head sideways. "Quiet," he commanded, "I hear something!"

The sound of gravel crunching under large tires reached their ears. Michael and AJ peered out the front window. A pair of small round red tail lights appeared through the fog. As Michael strained his eyes he began to make out the outline of a dark, box shaped vehicle just a few yards ahead. Then the tiny tail lights flashed brightly as the vehicle stopped. A door slammed and a shadowy, male figure approached through the fog. The man moved quickly to the rear of the vehicle and hunkered over. He seemed to be attaching a rope or strap to the large rear bumper of the vehicle. Michael surmised that the stylish,

continental-type spare tire and wooden tail gate were that of a 1951 Ford Woody.

Then the figure moved quickly to the front of Michael's car and wrapped the other end of the strap around the Plymouth's bumper brackets. As he leaned forward, Michael's headlights illuminated him, revealing an oddly familiar hat. The man then scrambled back into the Woody. Black smoke belched from the rear and dirt and rocks flew as the rear tires dug in. The bulky wagon jerked forward and snapped the tow rope taut.

"Give it the gas again, Michael!" urged AJ.

Nick responded from his precarious perch. "No, no! You might cause the car to rock again!"

"We can't just sit here like this..." screamed Michael, "I'm going for it!"

The tow rope continued to strain as Michael once again jammed the floor shifter into low. He gunned it and released the clutch. Suddenly, the Plymouth began to scrape forward over the earth mound. Then they could feel the rear wheels digging in as a shower of rocks and dirt flew over the precipice. Then came a terrific shock as the rear end bounced up and over the embankment. The loose earth on the other side stopped the car's tires and killed the roar of the small-block motor. Nick's legs were dragging across the ground and he lost his handhold on the door. He tumbled backwards across the rocky dirt. Even though he was obviously back on solid ground, he immediately jumped up, dove into the front seat and slammed the door.

As the three boys sat recovering their composure, the strange man jumped quickly out of the Woody. He untied the strap and without looking back, slid into the front seat of the wagon.

Michael hung his head out the window. "Hey, fella, thanks a lot! You saved our lives!"

There was no response as the old car slowly pulled away. The Plymouth's headlights blazed across the Woodie's personalized license plate. It read...*Kahuna*.

The boys still trembled slightly as they sat in their cafe booth. The waitress filled their coffee cups for the second time. They were still unnerved by the strange incident.

Michael stared intently at Nick. Something inside him had turned – like a switch. His conscious, rational mind was battling for control, trying to dispel what he knew deep within him was really the truth.

"I know what you're thinking...it's magic...right? I'm sick of hearing about all that magic shit!"

"Oh...okay! Are you going to tell us that you didn't experience being pulled away from oblivion by that old guy and his Woody...huh?" asked Nick.

Nick thumped his blunt index finger on the table. He glowered at Michael.

"You gonna tell us we all imagined that?"

"So some weirdo helped us...so what! I gunned it and that's how we got outta there!" replied Michael carefully.

Nick shook his head as Michael continued.

"The friggin' tires caught in the dirt, and that's your magic?" Michael paused for effect. "As for that Woody, it just happened to be driving by...that's all!"

"Michael," Nick implored, "don't fight it! Just accept it!"

AJ had been quiet during their argument. Finally he spoke up.

"Who was he?" asked AJ. He raised his voice. "Who was that guy? Man, this is crazy! I mean he, came out of nowhere! He pulls us off that cliff...then blasts off. Doesn't even wait around to see if we're okay. I don't get it!" AJ looked dazed. "Maybe I'm the one who's bonkers!"

Michael laughed. "I think you're both bonkers! And if we're gonna get to the campground tonight, we'd better get going. The girls will be waiting for us." Michael stood. "I'm gonna check the car while its in the parking lot and we have some light. It could have gotten damaged."

He left the restaurant.

Nick stood and withdrew his wallet. He pulled out two dollars and placed the tip on the table. AJ continued to stare straight ahead.

"You coming, AJ?" asked Nick.

"I'm getting tired of this, mate! Too many strange things have been happening. And now, Michael, acting like a bloody wanker." AJ gazed out toward the parking lot. "Sometimes I wish I had never left Australia."

Nick studied his friends rugged face. "I'm glad you did, mate!" said Nick.

AJ looked at Nick and grinned good-naturedly as Nick snatched up the check. AJ stood, and they headed for the cash register.

Moon Shadows

The strange fog retreated, revealing a beautiful star-filled night sky as the boys continued south on Highway 1. It was nine PM when they finally arrived at Redwood State Park. The moon was visible through the tips of the towering redwoods and the calm night air was warm and balmy. The boys pulled into their assigned campsite and spotted Monica, Andi and Andi's friend Lisa. They sat in a half circle around a flickering camp fire.

After a hasty greeting they prepared a dinner of hot dogs, pork and beans and Pepsi. They settled in around the crackling fire.

Everyone engaged in friendly conversation, toasted marshmallows and drank hot chocolate. The group was lively, except for Michael. He remained silent and withdrawn.

Group laughter rang out over something that AJ said. Monica looked over at Michael. She touched his hand lovingly.

"What's wrong, Michael?" she asked.

He observed Monica as she crouched next to him on the low log. The glow of the firelight ignited the golden highlights in her hair. Monica was about five-feet four inches tall, with thick chestnut-colored hair that she wore long. It fell well past her shoulders and down over slim, deeply tanned shoulders. She had beautiful features and a smile that revealed flawless white teeth. Her skin had a natural healthy glow and she wore very little make-up. She did not need it. She was classically beautiful, which had attracted Michael to her in the first place.

"Oh, nothing," replied Michael, recovering from his rapture. He grasped Monica's hand and she slid closer to him, nuzzling her fragrant face into the space between his neck and shoulder.

"We could go to my tent," she purred, looking up at Michael. She raised her eyebrows impishly.

Michael's solemn expression changed. He smiled.

"That's the best news I've had all day!"

After a moment, Michael stood and stretched dramatically. He feigned a great yawn.

"Well, goodnight all, see ya in the morning," he announced.

His wrapped his arm around Monica's waist and led her through the darkness to her tent. The rest of the group continued sitting around the campfire. Then Andi spoke.

"What's the matter with Michael tonight? He's so out of it. Normally he's the life of the party."

"We had a kind of weird experience this evening on the way down Coast Highway 1," explained Nick.

"I'll say we did!" piped AJ.

"What do you mean...weird?" asked Andi. She looked inquisitively from Nick to AJ.

"Well," began Nick, "it all kind of started one morning at breakfast after surfing..."

Nick proceeded to enumerate the series of strange incidents and encounters that they had experienced. Andi and Lisa sat spellbound as he detailed the events, ending with the car crash and their brush with death earlier that evening. The group went silent as each tried to interpret the meaning of the strange happenings.

Inside the tent, Monica slipped into the sleeping bag. She shivered a little as her bare feet came in contact with the cool, inner nylon liner. Mostly, Monica felt anticipation of her and Michael finally being alone together.

They had met two years ago at a beach party. Monica was with Andi that evening and Michael was with Nick. That night they hit it off as if they had known each other for years. She was immediately drawn to his mannerisms. He seemed to be slightly shy, but confident at the same time. He was average in size, about five-feet eleven, and slim. Although he was not big or muscular, he projected a sense of strength and vitality. She especially loved his dark brown hair, which he wore long. It had gold and red highlights and curled slightly as it followed the contour of his head. His dark brown eyes could peer into her very soul and with a simple glance he seemed to know if something was bothering her. Tonight, however, something was bothering him.

She watched him slide his legs into the large bag. She moved slightly to allow him room. He moved his lean body in easily and ended up resting on one elbow, looking into her limpid blue-green eyes. He gazed at the beautiful features of her face, her high cheekbones, soft upturned nose. Her full lips glowed with a natural red-violet color. He stroked her long flowing hair, then leaned forward and kissed her.

"Sorry about tonight," he said, still threading his fingers through her soft hair. "This is just what I need. You and me together...alone."

Monica fingered the short curls on the back of his neck as she searched into the depths of his dark eyes.

"Do you want to tell me about it?" she whispered.

"Later!" replied Michael huskily as he pulled her close and kissed her. It was a long kiss and Monica wrapped her arms firmly around his neck. The nylon bag began to bulge and make whispery sounds as they rolled over gently in a close embrace. Soon they caressed each other as Michael ran his hand down to the small of her back and massaged gently. He pressed her tightly against him.

"Geeze Monica," breathed Michael, "you feel so good."

The campfire was beginning to die now and no one made a move to add wood.

"Oh, Nick," purred Andi, moving closer to him and threading her arm through his. She pressed her firm bosom against his triceps.

"Thank God you're all right. You must have been scared to death," she whispered.

"I guess I was," replied Nick. "But you know, it's just been so weird!" He paused again. "I keep thinking about that strange old Woody, plus all the other bizarre things that have happened to us in the past few days. It's as if someone's trying to tell us something."

Nick rubbed his forehead with the palm of his right hand.

"What does it all mean?" he asked the night.

Andi smiled sweetly. "Maybe they are telling you something, but you aren't listening."

"What do you mean not listening?" replied Nick incredulously. "It's all I've been thinking about for the past several days."

Andi's smile transformed into an expression of gentle understanding. "Well...I can't tell you what to do," she replied. "But what's happening to you guys seems real and it seems to be something personal between them...and the three of you."

Nick laughed. "You're a great help!"

He picked up a stick and began to draw a series of horizontal lines in the dirt.

Andi laughed, "Well, sorry, duuude, but I've got my own problems!"

Nick raised his eyebrows in surprise and looked at Andi. She continued.

"I have nowhere to sleep! Michael and Monica have taken over my tent."

Nick smiled back mischievously.

"Oh, don't worry your pretty head," he consoled theatrically. His arm slithered around her waist as he looked into her eyes. Suddenly his expression changed. He removed his arm from behind her, clasped his hands together and stared straight ahead.

"What's wrong, Nick?" she asked in surprise.

"Nothing," he replied flatly, "you and Lisa can share the other tent. AJ and I will sleep by the fire in our bags."

AJ suddenly came alive.

"Eh, what was that, mate?" he asked incredulously.

Nick looked at AJ and shook his head slightly.

AJ spoke again. "Hey matey...can we talk this over?"

Nick got up and offered a hand to Andi. AJ stared at him intently, but he ignored him.

"I'll walk you home," said Nick.

Andi and Lisa glanced at each other briefly, then Andi took Nick's hand. He helped her up from the log and they turned and walked off in the direction of the tent. When they reached the tent, Nick stopped and drew her close. As he kissed her, Andi wrapped her arms tightly around his neck.

"Thank you, Nick," she purred as she hugged him. "Goodnight," he whispered softly.

They kissed again.

Andi pulled away and slipped into the tent leaving him standing alone in the darkness. After a moment, he turned and returned in the direction of the fire.

AJ and Lisa stepped slowly along the path, through the soft fire light. Lisa had jet-black hair that bounced when she walked. Her dark eyebrows and long lashes accented her fiery blue eyes. She was about five-feet three inches tall, with a petite figure. They stopped in the darkness. AJ smiled apologetically and reached around her waist.

"Well...I don't know what to say," he stuttered.

Lisa put her arms around his waist and pulled him close. They kissed, then she pushed him gently away.

"Don't say anything, AJ," she suggested.

"I don't know what's gotten into Nick lately," continued AJ.

"Oh, AJ," replied Lisa, "I think he's sweet. You could take a lesson from him," she teased.

AJ moved away from her.

"What's that suppose to mean?" he asked. "Am I such an animal?"

"Oh, no!" replied Lisa. "But it's nice to be treated like a lady."

AJ could not believe his ears.

"A lady!" he screeched. "I thought you Sheilas wanted to be treated equal."

There was a long pause as Lisa examined him in the dim light.

"AJ, I'm not a feminist or a Sheila, whatever that is, but I like to be treated nice. And you know what? I'll do the same for you and that's what I call equal treatment."

AJ grinned mischievously as he spoke in a hushed voice.

"Hey, there's always the car."

"Oh, AJ!" scolded Lisa.

Then she broke the bad news to him. "AJ...I won't be able to continue on the trip. I drove here in my mother's car and she needs it back for tomorrow. I have to return home in the morning."

AJ's face drooped perceptibly in the dim light. A little boy smile spread across his face and he hugged her tightly. "Aw well...that's just my damn luck, isn't it," he said. "Come on...lady," said AJ, "I'll walk you to your tent. You've got a long drive ahead of you tomorrow and I need me beauty sleep so I can surf properly."

Inside the other tent Monica lay sleeping peacefully in Michael's arms. Michael, however, was anything but peaceful. His body flinched restlessly and his eyes darted wildly beneath their lids. The silhouette of his face stood out razor sharp against the dimly lit tent wall. He was in the midst of a dream. A dream that was becoming increasingly frequent and familiar. First, he perceived the purple darkness that slowly changed to paynes gray. It mixed with the earthy yellow of morning light. He felt the caress of a warm offshore breeze and smelled a mixture of fragrant tropical scents. As he squinted in the dim light he could discern the outline of coconut palms swaying in a soft breeze. Then came the sound of drums, Hawaiian music and waves crashing.

He turned his head to the right. In the velvet darkness of an alcove of banana plants and palm trees he saw three men huddled around a glowing beach fire. The fire flared suddenly, revealing the tall Hawaiian man who stood behind the others in the shadows. Michael stared intently at this man. Suddenly his sleeping mind made an important realization.

"That's Duke Kahanamoku!" he confirmed.

As kids, Nick's dad, Joe, used to show them old photographs of himself as a boy at Waikiki with the Duke. In one particular photo, Duke stood with Joe. In this strange reverie, however, the three men kneeled on one leg in front of The Duke, as if posing for a photograph. His mind's eye slowly panned the group from left to right, stopping on the man at the Duke's right. This man wore a floppy hat that concealed his features.

Suddenly, the campfire flared intensely and the four men slowly dissolved away. Michael could hear laughter through the brightness. Slowly, he began to distinguish the figures of several men surfing. He spotted the Duke riding an ancient redwood Hot Curl surfboard. He stood straight and tall as he streaked along on a six-foot wave. Three other surfers rode 60's style longboards. They began maneuvering back and forth, cruising along together, happily sharing the same wave.

Michael's body reflexed convulsively. Monica's head was resting on his shoulder. Michael jerked himself upright.

"Eeeek!" she shrieked, in reaction to the rude awakening.

Michael panted next to her. She touched his sweat soaked body.

"What's the matter, Michael?" she asked sleepily.

"Oh, it's nothing," he replied, "just a dream."

Surfin' Safari

Michael, Nick and AJ sat on the expansive white sand beach. They watched the glassy morning swells roll in next to the quaint pier, splashing against the pilings until reaching shore. It was a typical crowded south coast mess with a mix of longboarders, shortboarders, boogie boarders and even a few kayaks thrown in for good measure. It was the same frustrating scene, no matter where they went.

"Hey...isn't that Kevin Mathews?" asked Nick. "Yeah, that has to be!" he confirmed. "I'd know his style anywhere."

"Best Goofy-foot around," replied Michael.

"Yeah, look at the power of his drop-knee turn and that fan of water he throws out when he cuts back," said Nick. They all hooted.

"Who-hooo!"

"He's good all right," confirmed AJ, watching for a reaction from his friends, "for a longboarder!"

Nick threw a piece of seaweed at him. He ducked.

"You jealous, AJ?" countered Michael, displaying an equally toothy grin.

"You wish," replied AJ, pointing out Jake Morris. "Now there's a *real* surfer...rides huge waves and he's only sixteen years old. Shreds on shortboards as well as longboards."

"Yeah, but everyone knows that the classic contemporary longboarder of today is Bobby Winger," confirmed Michael. "And he's never ridden a shortboard!" Michael chuckled and glanced back at AJ. "In fact, some people think my style is a lot like his."

"Bloody hell too," cackled AJ.

"I like to watch Mikey Del Grecco, longboard," replied Nick, "he's got the ultimate classic-contemporary mix if you ask me. And he's Italian!"

The boys continued to sit on the cool sand and watch. They pointed out the various local surfers and what they liked and didn't like about each of them.

"Hope the girls get here soon," said Michael finally.

"Give 'em time," replied Nick. "Monica had to call her parents and check in...they'll show up. Hey, they couldn't be too far behind us."

"Look at that board!" said AJ as a young man walked past them. He gripped a gleaming new shortboard under his arm.

"What a beaut," remarked AJ, "been thinking of splurging and getting a new board."

"Get with it, kook!" joked Michael. "Get a longboard!"

AJ opened his mouth but before he could reply, the girls interrupted from behind. They plopped down unceremoniously onto the sand.

"Hi, guys!" said Monica, kneeling on all fours. She leaned forward deliberately close to Michael.

Michael smiled broadly and pulled her close. "Hi, babe," he replied, kissing her.

"How come you're not out surfing?" she asked.

"We've just been sitting here, checking it out," replied Michael, "It's small and crowded."

Andi had become preoccupied with observing Michael and Monica. She turned her head toward Nick. He was looking at her. His face brightened.

"Hi, beautiful," cooed Nick.

Andi scooted across the sand to where Nick sat. He put his arm around her shoulder.

"Hi, there you surfer hunk," she said and brushed her lips against his cheek. Andi noticed

AJ. He sat alone with his arms wrapped around his knees.

"Uh...AJ," stammered Andi. "Sorry about Lisa. She really wanted to come along...felt real bad."

"No worries mate, we'll catch up later," replied AJ.

She giggled at his accent.

Suddenly Michael jumped up, "C'mon you guys, let's get wet!"

He grabbed a towel, wrapped it around his waist and began pulling off his clothes as if he were being timed. Within seconds his pants dropped to the sand and the breeze caught his Da Bull T-shirt as he flung it over his head. He stepped into his farmer john wetsuit and began wiggling it up over his hips. The suit was called a Farmer John because it had long legs and a bib-type top, like denim overalls. It was an old O'Neill suit that he had purchased at a garage sale. Michael loved the suit because it allowed his upper body so much freedom of movement. It was smooth black neoprene, with a nylon liner and an old O'Neill logo stenciled on the right breast. He had never seen another suit like it and felt special when he wore it.

AJ and Nick got the hint. It finally dawned on them that Michael was going to beat them into the water and out to the surf. As if on cue, they jumped up and began stripping off their clothes. AJ unrolled his suit from a dark blue water-soaked towel. As it fell to the sand it made a raspy sound. It was wet from the previous day's use and had spent the night in the trunk of Michael's car. White sand coated its outside like sugar frosting on a donut. He uncoiled it, pulled out the arms and legs. It smelled musty and stale. He pulled it up over his thighs, toward his waist.

"Yaahh," he screeched, "this bloody thing is clammy!"

He thrust his arms into the sleeves and leveraged the suit upwards. His hands slipped through the cuffs and the neoprene flexed as it popped over his upper torso. Wet, smelly sand flew all over the girls. He squirmed hideously inside the suit.

"Ooo...yuk!" complained Andi, as she wiped wet sand from her face.

"Sorry, but this bloody girdle is so clammy I can't stand it!" replied AJ.

"Aw, quit complaining you damn Aussie," teased Nick.

"Yeah," added Michael, "these down-under guys can't handle wearing the neoprene. Blood's thin from too many years of tropical pampering!"

Michael whisked up his board and ran down toward the water. He waded in about knee deep, then began biding his time as he waited for Nick and AJ. He scooped a handful of wet sand and rubbed it vigorously into the thickly beaded wax that coated the deck of his surfboard. The sand scratched the glazed top coating of wax and made the surface tacky. Michael glanced back to see what was keeping his friends. He knew the drill. Paddling out together was part of the surfing ritual. Soon Nick and AJ splashed into the shore break and they began a paddle race into the line-up.

Monica and Andi sat and watched the boys cavort in the surf. Due to the crowded conditions, it became necessary to share any waves they might catch. They put aside any frustration that they might have felt. Their mood became playful.

Michael quickly paddled out and caught the first wave. He dropped in and rode along with several other surfers. A kayak soon joined them. Suddenly, Michael went straight off and aimed his board for Nick who was paddling out. At the last second he dove, grabbed Nick around the waist and wrestled him from his board. They rolled about in the small breakers like two sea-otters at play. AJ moved in and grabbed Michael's loose board. He lay his foot on the deck and began paddling away, towing it behind him.

"Hey!" yelled Michael. He broke Nick's headlock and began swimming after AJ. He swam smooth and sure, alternating his stroke from crawl to butterfly. He closed the distance quickly and within moments, caught AJ. Another wrestling match ensued as Michael pulled him into the water.

Monica and Andi continued to watch with amusement.

Suddenly Andi became serious. "Has Michael said anything about what's been happening to them?" she asked.

"No," replied Monica arching her eyebrows. "Just what they told us at the camp fire last night."

Andi proceeded to detail the incidents starting with the first morning at the cafe and ending with the near brush with death on Highway 1.

"My God...no wonder Nick was so shook up last night!" exclaimed Monica.

Andi looked at her with concern. "Poor Nick, how terrible! I wonder what it all means?"

"I wish I knew," replied Monica. "They seem to be so preoccupied all the time. Oh well, the waves look like fun. Think I'll go out for a while...care to join me?"

"No, you go ahead," replied Andi, "I feel like just sitting here and watching."

As Monica prone paddled her surfboard toward the boys, she watched Nick catch a wave. Then Michael dropped in on him and motioned for Nick to join him. Nick stepped forward onto Michael's surfboard and left his empty surfboard to ghost ride. He and Michael now cruised along, riding tandem, on the small wave. AJ spotted them and as they passed him, he caught the broken part of the wave. He stood quickly and pumped his board until he was directly behind them. AJ surprised Nick as he leaped onto the rear of the board. For the next five seconds they all cruised along on Michael's board. Soon, however, AJ's surfboard, still tethered by his leash, began to drag them down from behind. He clutched at Nick and Nick grabbed Michael. They all went careening comically into the crashing wave.

As Nick swam after his board, AJ paddled across to where Monica sat watching. He pulled up next to her and they watched Michael ride another wave.

"That was a beauty, mate!" hooted AJ.

"Thanks, yer old bloke!" Michael shouted as he paddled past them effortlessly.

"You know, surfing seems to bring everything into perspective. Gets rid of the cobwebs, you know?" said Monica to AJ.

"Sure does, Monica," he replied. "Lets join em."

Monica nodded and went prone as they began to paddle toward Nick and Michael.

During this time a group of young locals was sitting just inside from them. They watched and listened to their conversation. One rather large, blond haired boy with a sneer on his face suddenly blurted out, "F—kin longboarders!" loud enough for the boys to hear.

"Hey AJ," joked Michael, "you sure you want to hang around with us f—kin' longboarders?"

They laughed brusquely as Michael caught another wave and rode it all the way to shore. Nick caught the next wave and went in also. Monica turned to AJ.

"I guess we're leaving, AJ," said Monica. "See you up on the beach."

She turned and caught a small wave and left AJ sitting alone. He bobbed there with his arms folded across his chest. He was thinking about Lisa and waiting for a wave to take in. His thoughts were rudely interrupted.

"Hey...*mate!*" jeered the blond leader. "Why don't you Helgy's go home...go crowd your own waters?"

While the rude assailant waited for a response from AJ, his friends glanced at each other and snickered. The young punk continued. "We got enough cowboys surfin' our break without having to deal with f—kin' foreign geeks too!"

AJ had tried to ignore the guy, but now felt compelled to respond.

"Yeah, It's pretty obvious," replied AJ as he eyed the group, "there are a lot of cowboys around here all right...matey."

A wave now approached, so AJ turned and paddled for it. He stood and began riding toward shore. As AJ passed, the local turned and caught the broken part of the wave. He started gyrating madly in an attempt to reach AJ. He moved up quickly and at the last second before the wave broke, he dove for AJ. The local missed and did a comical belly-flop on the flat trough of the wave. The wave broke over him and seconds later he surfaced.

"You're dead meat, man!" screamed the local. "Dead meat!"

When AJ reached the beach, he walked past the others without speaking. Michael and Nick looked out toward where the pack of locals sat. They could hear their hoarse screams. Just then, Monica walked up. She moved close to Michael.

"Lets go get some dinner," said Michael and they left the beach.

Bally-hoo

The "Bally-hoo" night club was located in the quaint sea-side community of Pismo Beach. It was crowded and noisy as a local rock band ground out a tune in the background. The male vocalist reached high, squealing forth inaudible and unrecognizable lyrics. Back in the early sixties, at the height of the surfing craze in California, Dick Dale and the Del-Tones played at the Bally-hoo quite regularly.

Nick, Michael, AJ, Monica and Andi squeezed into a booth near the kitchen door. They were in good spirits as the band began playing one of Monica's favorite songs. She looked at Michael and he moved close and kissed her. Nick and Andi cuddled. Their heads joined and they spoke in quiet tones, accented by an occasional giggle. AJ sat alone, fidgeting and glancing around self-consciously.

"Gee, AJ, too bad about, Lisa," reiterated Andi.

"No worries, mate...wish the food would get here," he replied defensively.

Suddenly AJ grasped the clear Lucite dinner special stand from the table and began examining it.

"What are you doing?" asked Andi, still watching him.

AJ's face broke into a wicked smile.

"The chef's special, huh!" he remarked. He fidgeted nervously as he removed the black and white printed card insert. Everyone watched as AJ flipped the advertisement over and exposed the blank backside. AJ emitted a fiendish laugh. "Heee, heee, haww...does anyone have a pen?" he inquired.

Lisa fumbled through her small purse and produced a retractable ball point pen. "Will this do?" she asked.

"He...he...heee!" cackled AJ again as he snatched the pen from her palm and went immediately to work on the paper.

"What are you drawing this time, AJ?" asked Nick.

AJ glanced up quickly, "You'll see," he cackled. As he sketched away he continued to make occasional comments and emit small hideous giggles. Finally, he motioned his arms in a gesture of finality and stuffed the paper back into its clear plastic stand. He rotated his handiwork slowly and deliberately, displaying it to each eager face. The table erupted in uncontrolled laughter. Tucked neatly inside the plastic holder was a beautiful rendition of an overweight man, dressed in an apron and chef's hat. He held a large platter containing a pair of steaming polka-dot boxer shorts garnished with potatoes, carrots and gravy. Across the top the caption read, "Today's Special – The Chef's Shorts."

They passed the drawing around the table for a closer inspection. Spasmodic laughter continued. At that moment the waitress arrived with their orders. She became curious and immediately spotted the modified dinner special menu.

"What's that?" she asked Nick. "Do you mind if I see it?" She did not wait for a response as she reached over his shoulder and snatched it from his hands. AJ sat across from Nick, looking like the cat caught with the canary.

"Whose art?" she asked.

AJ timidly raised his hand.

She was silent for several moments as she held the drawing close to her face and studied it carefully. She lowered it and looked straight into his eyes. AJ was expecting the worst. A large toothy grin spread across her face.

"Hooo-Haa-Haa-Hooo...this is great!" she cackled in staccato. "I gotta show this to Pete!"

AJ's expression transformed from concern to startled vexation as he watched the waitress scurry away. She continued to giggle hysterically as she cradled the menu stand in her hands and burst through the swinging kitchen doors. AJ was certain that in the next millisecond the chef would come roaring out of the kitchen spouting profanities and demanding an immediate apology. Sounds began to emanate from the kitchen.

"Hee-hee-hoo-hoo-haaa!"

"They're all laughing in there!" exclaimed Andi.

Soon, a big man wearing a chef's hat leaned through the kitchen order pick-up counter. He peered toward their table. He was a robust man with a wide friendly face and a big smile. The waitress pulled him back into the kitchen and pointed toward their table as she whispered something in his ear. AJ acknowledged them as he smiled and waved his hand timidly.

The friends could no longer contain themselves. They exploded into uncontrolled laughter. Like an echo, more chortles rang out from the kitchen. The kitchen doors burst open and the waitress emerged in a flurry. She came straight over to their table and began to refill their coffee cups.

"Pete is the owner," she explained, "he likes the art...says he's going to get it framed and hang it up in the kitchen!" She moved skillfully from cup to cup. "We all think it looks just like him! Hee-haaa-haaa-hoooo!"

The food was warm and delicious and they all dug in hungrily. As AJ ate he occasionally cast a bewildered glance toward the kitchen. Then he scanned from the kitchen, toward the large dance floor and the other side of the large room. Suddenly his eyes stopped. There was a pretty girl sitting in a booth with two other girls. She seemed to be watching him and smiled when their eyes met. AJ felt conspicuous. This was too much attention in one night, even for him. He dropped his gaze. However, when he looked up moments later, her eyes were still upon him.

By now the band was back from their break and the music began again. Michael and Monica jumped up and left the table to dance. Nick looked at Andi.

"How 'bout it, Babe?" he asked.

She nodded her approval and they left as well, leaving AJ alone at the table. He began to feel the nervous fidgets returning. He looked across the room once again. The pretty girl seemed to sense AJ's eyes and looked up. He knew that it was now or never. He must make his move or leave now and go sit in the car. After a moment of reflection, AJ stood. He fixed his attention on the girl and proceeded to give his rendition of John Travolta in a scene from "Saturday Night Fever." After a series of exaggerated, rotary gyrations of his lower torso he lifted his arms gracefully and gestured, toreador style over his head. He thrust his index fingers in exaggerated movements, pointing toward her and then the dance floor. To his amazement, she smiled and nodded back enthusiastically. AJ quickly crossed the room.

"Hello...I'm AJ...care to dance?" he asked.

"Sure," she replied. Her blue eyes flashed a smile.

AJ led her to the dance floor.

"Neat band," he screamed over the amplified music.

"Uh-huh," said the young girl, nodding back and smiling again.

They danced through several songs as AJ whooped it up. He glanced back at the table and noticed Michael watching them with interest. AJ signaled with two thumbs up. Michael smiled and returned the gesture.

AJ would not allow his lame foot to prevent him from having a good time. He danced with his new friend until the band stopped to allow the lead singer to have a break.

"Would you like to join me at our table?" he asked.

The girl nodded and turned toward her friends. She waved and they got the idea as AJ led her away. He helped her into the booth on one side and slid into the other. They pressed themselves into a booth made to accommodate four people.

"This is Toni, you guys," said AJ.

The group acknowledged Toni, then went back to their conversation. Just then, the band started up again and began to play a familiar tune. Once again, AJ became consumed with excitement. He took Toni by the hand.

"Want to dance?" he asked breathlessly. She smiled and nodded as AJ helped her from the snug booth.

The singer stood off-stage sipping from a tall drink as the band rocked-out a familiar surfing instrumental from the sixties. AJ began his version of an aborigine fertility dance. He zigged his neck back and forth as he stepped along to the beat of the song. Suddenly, he heard a harsh voice bark from behind and felt warm breath against his neck.

"Hey, mate...or should I say meat...dead meat!".

It was the young surf-hood that AJ had the altercation with earlier. The intruder squeezed between Toni and AJ and his two sleazy friends closed in from either side. The punk pressed his sunburned face close. The stench of cheap aftershave invaded AJ's sinus cavities.

"Did you hear me, Kook!" exclaimed the punk, "you geeks drop into our town – surf our spots – plus you think you can just nab our chicks too?"

He shoved AJ backwards into the two sleazes, who caught him and pushed him from side-to-side. They now surrounded AJ in a crude circle. AJ could feel his anger growing, but sensed that he was seriously outnumbered. Nevertheless, he stood his ground and leered back dangerously at them. Meanwhile, Toni backed away and scurried back to the booth.

"I think AJ is in trouble," Toni shouted frantically to the others, then she left to join her friends across the room.

They turned in unison to observe AJ on the dance floor. Nick and Michael glanced at each other, slid out of the booth and moved quickly away. As they approached, they could see the young punk shoving AJ again. He was yelling something in his face. Michael walked up behind the guy and tapped him on the shoulder.

"Hey you!" said Michael calmly.

The blond youth turned and faced Michael. He sneered.

Michael continued. "We don't want to start any trouble here, so why don't you just drop it?"

The local grabbed Michael's shirt with both hands and twisted, drawing Michael close. Then he looked at his friends. "The Kook wants me to drop it," he said mockingly. Then he turned back to

Michael. His bulging blood-shot eyes glowered menacingly. "How 'bout I drop you, geek, right here!"

Michael's features began to transform from friendly, to focused, intense and dangerous. The sensation of anger rushed over him like a biological fuel injector. All his senses became alive, on alert. His hands clenched instinctively as tough sinewy fingers squeaked against callused palms. His oversized knuckles became white and popped loudly as his hands tightened into rock-like fists. Suddenly, an inner voice softly intervened.

"Never use karate in anger..." repeated the calm voice of Sensei Omi, "...use only to protect your friends, your loved ones or someone in need."

Michael's mind went into a flurry of thought. "Would this be one of those extreme situations that Sensei has trained me for all those years?" he thought. "Violence should always be a last resort and should be avoided if at all possible." He nodded imperceptibly as the anger within him dissipated. "I won't hurt them...I'll just disarm them."

AJ looked from Michael, then to Nick. "What do you think, mate?" he asked.

Nick's eyes moved from the young hood's fists clenching Michael's shirt, to Michael's face. He raised his eyebrows. "I think this guy has really got his hands full," replied Nick wryly.

Without warning, Michael swung his right arm in a smooth arc above his head. The room became quiet for Michael as he retreated into his inner self. He began to sense every movement, even to his side and rear. He felt as though he was observing the action from outside his body. Again he heard Omi's voice.

"Never allow anger to control your emotions, Michael-san. Use your opponent's anger against him and to your advantage."

His arm came down effortlessly and brushed the aggressor's hands from his shirt. Now he retreated slightly, and began to execute a series of blurred, noiseless movements. He drew his right arm in close, braced it with his left arm, then rotated like a human watch spring, uncoiling with incredible force. His right arm struck the intruder and lifted his feet from the dance floor, propelling him backwards. He flew into the arms of his friends and his momentum sent all three spinning across the dance floor. The surprise move angered them and they leaped up in unison and rushed back from every side. Michael's expression remained tranquil and focused as they attacked clumsily. He studied each attacker momentarily, then swiftly and cleanly disabled them. Nick and AJ watched, mouths gaping. The music droned on.

Nick cupped his hands and yelled into AJ's ear. "Do you think we ought to help him?"

"Nah," yelled AJ in reply, "I'm wearing me classic Greg Noll T-shirt."

The fighting continued until at one point the three managed to corner Michael.

"How bout now?" asked Nick.

They observed Michael, who was being held by two of the thugs as the third attempted to punch him in the stomach. Michael looked over at his friends.

"Feel free to jump in any time you guys," he yelled.

"Maybe we should," replied Nick playfully.

Suddenly the blond punk thrust his fist forward, aiming a punch toward Michael's face. At the last moment, Michael moved his head and evaded the blow. The fist continued on a trajectory and struck his friend squarely on the nose.

"Ooofffmmpp," the boy bellowed, as he absorbed the full force of the blow. "My nose is broken...you asshole!" He immediately released Michael and fell to the floor.

Now, with his hands free, Michael went into a series of dance-like movements that sent the other two hoods sprawling across the floor.

One by one they stood shakily and retreated through the side exit.

"Well, I guess he won't need our help after all," said Nick, winking at AJ.

Michael glanced venomously toward AJ and Nick as he brushed off his clothes and tucked in his favorite Aloha shirt. The shirt hung open, all the buttons were gone.

AJ and Nick flanked Michael and led him back to their table. Just then, the waitress arrived.

"We saw the whole thing!" she announced. "Those young punks cause trouble here all the time. Pete was pleased to see that they finally got what they deserved!"

She turned and disappeared back into the kitchen.

Michael looked at AJ and Nick.

"Thanks for the help, guys!" he said sarcastically.

"We were waiting for when you really needed us," said AJ. "Besides we need our energy for driving tonight and surfing tomorrow, mate."

AJ thrust out his chin toward Andi and Monica.

"Besides...you Sheilas wouldn't want this beautiful face marred in any way...now would you?" he grinned comically.

Andi and Monica laughed. This caused Michael to smile weakly. He draped Monica's leather jacket around her shoulders and she moved close to his face to examine a blue-red bubble that bulged just beneath his right eye. He flinched slightly as she probed it with her index finger.

"It's nothing...just a bruise," he assured her.

As they walked through the front entrance the waitress and Pete came out of the kitchen. The big man stood with a wide smile and folded arms as he watched the group leave. Pete shook his head, "Heh-heh...the chef's shorts!"

Outta Gas

Michael lowered his gaze from the highway that stretched out before him. His eyes fixed upon the radiant dial of his Seiko Submariner wrist watch.

"Eleven-thirty AM," he thought, "exactly one hour since I left Monica."

Just thinking about Monica made his stomach gurgle and his head get light. For various reasons, the girls had to return to Santa Lina.

"Oh well...what the hell," thought Michael, "this was a surfin' safari. And besides, the trip probably wouldn't have been much fun for the girls anyhow." Michael felt his stomach muscles tighten. He was experiencing a growing sense that this trip was very important. He would miss Monica, but something was compelling him to push onward. Something that he did not understand. Something that simultaneously drew him closer and repelled him away. Like the feeling he got when he surfed big waves. He glanced back at his watch. His dad had brought it home from a business trip to Japan several years ago. His dad would always bring a gift for he and his brother, James, when ever he went on a long trip. I guess it was his way of making up for the divorce. None of the gifts ever really meant much to Michael, however, except for this watch. It kept perfectly accurate time, it was waterproof and it looked real cool with its stainless steel band, blue coral face and silver bezel. Whether or not his father ever realized it, that watch was the most thoughtful thing he had ever done for Michael. His knuckles protruded as he gripped the laminated wood sports steering wheel. He wondered if his father would even care if he knew how much the gift had meant to him.

The Formula "S" Barracuda cruised effortlessly over the desolate country road. The efficient, powerful 273 cubic inch motor developed 230 horsepower and got twenty-two miles-per-gallon. The factory resonator dual exhaust system emitted a throaty roar as they climbed, dipped and wove through the hilly countryside. Highway 1 was an alternate route to Highway 101 and Michael had chosen it because it spent most of the time near the Pacific as it wound its way south.

Nick sat in front on the passenger side. His expression was one of apprehension as he stared with unfocused eyes at the blur of changing countryside that raced past his window. As usual, AJ was sound asleep in the back seat.

"Look Michael...I still think we should have headed for home," said Nick. "I'm just about broke."

"What's at home?" asked Michael. "Monica and Andi are going to Los Angeles with Andi's mother, for three days."

"My mom will be worried," added Nick.

"Call her," said Michael quickly.

"I haven't seen a phone for a couple of hours," replied Nick. "For that matter, I haven't seen anything for hours. Where the hell are we anyway?"

He looked out the front window, then from side to side.

"Haven't we been on this road once already?"

"We must have been, at some time in our lives," replied Michael.

There was a long pause. "I'm going on instinct," replied Michael. "Something looks familiar and I follow it. I feel like we should keep heading south...it just feels right"

Nick looked intently at Michael. His face muscles began to tighten visibly. He stared for long moments.

"Okay...what is it, Michael?" asked Nick. "I know you, dude, and you've been acting weird these past few days."

Michael looked straight ahead without replying. He was considering Nick's words and thinking of a way to express his feelings. Finally, he faced Nick.

"Look, I know this is gonna sound weird, but...I don't really know where I'm going, okay? We're heading south on Highway 1 and it feels right. I just have to keep going...that's all. I don't even know where we'll end up, but it's a surfin' safari, right?"

The dubious expression on Nick's face was a dead giveaway.

"It'll be okay," continued Michael, glancing at Nick again. "We'll just camp on the beach."

"I still think we should go home," replied Nick.

There were sounds of rustling and grunting from the back seat. Nick glanced back just as AJ's head popped up. AJ yawned theatrically.

"Where are we?" asked AJ, craning his neck around quizzically.

"It's about time, Romeo," replied Nick with a smile. "If you wouldn't spend all your time chasing women..."

AJ didn't respond. He just continued to look around.

"Where the hell are we, mate?" he asked again. "I thought we were going home!"

Suddenly the car began to sputter, lost power and coasted to a stop. Michael yanked it over onto the gravel shoulder. He swore repeatedly under his breath as he tried to restart the car's engine. It cranked but there was no response from what had always been a very lively and dependable Plymouth engine.

"Damn it. I told you that we should have just gone home. What now?" exclaimed Nick.

Michael's hands gripped the top of the steering wheel. He rested his forehead on them, then slowly rolled his head until he faced Nick.

"What do you normally do when you run out of gas?" replied Michael, smiling sickly.

"Out of gas!" shrieked Nick. "We passed a station just a few miles back! Why didn't you stop there if the car was low?"

Michael pondered the question.

"Did you see the price of that gas? It was fifty cents a gallon more than the station in San Luis. They think they can get away with robbing people because they're the only stations around...screw them!"

"Yeah, screw them," replied Nick ironically, "now we have to walk back to the station and they'll still screw us! You should have filled-up the car in San Luis."

Once again Michael contemplated his friend. The smile left his face.

"You know as well as I do that my gas tank will only hold about seven gallons!" said Michael.

As Nick listened he recalled the night that they were at Nick's house, changing a tire on

Michael's car. Nick had carelessly placed his father's floor jack under the rear of the Barracuda and proceeded to jack away. Unknown to Michael, Nick had placed the lift arm under the gas tank. As Michael changed the tire he commented to AJ that he could hear a sizzling sound. AJ walked around until he finally traced it to the car's racing style, quick-release gas filler pipe. He unlatched the chrome cap and was instantly blown backwards by an explosion of air and gas vapor. As the compressed vapor escaped, the gas tank crushed upward. There was a loud scrunch as the car came down. Michael's toes were nearly crushed between the rear brake drum and the cement driveway. The remarkable thing is that when AJ landed some ten feet from the car, he still had a lit Marlboro cigarette in his mouth. If it had ignited the gas vapors, the explosion would have blown them all sky high.

"I wonder where the closest gas station is?" asked Nick smiling sheepishly.

"About seven miles back, mates," replied Michael, "the screw job station." Michael lifted his left eyebrow and gazed from Nick to AJ.

"I think we're gonna have to push," he announced.

"No way," complained Nick. "I'm not pushing!"

"Okay...okay," insisted Michael. "I'm not gonna leave my car out on this deserted road. I'll push it!"

Nick sucked the fresh country air in through his nose as he leaned forward. Beads of sweat rolled from the short hair on the back of his neck and dripped onto the gray-blue pavement that passed beneath the car.

"Why do we allow ourselves to be talked into these things?" he whined.

"Because, we're a couple of wankers!" suggested AJ.

"I'll tell you this," continued Nick, "this is the last time! He's not gonna talk me into this crap...ever again!"

As Nick puffed along, oxygen-rich blood tunneled its way into the peripherals of his brain, exciting mental activity. Whenever Nick exercised strenuously he would be besieged by a flood of random thoughts, ideas and memories. As he struggled along, he recalled a story that his dad had once told him about an old Woody station wagon he had owned in 1961. He could almost hear his father, Joe, speak as the memory played back through his mind's eye.

"It was a '51 Ford Woody that was pretty much stripped down...had no seats! The car had originally belonged to a guy named Kevin Kottle. Kevin worked at the local junk yard in Santa Lina, which was where your Uncle Dave and I used to get most of our car parts. Kevin was a kind of a surfer-hodad. He wanted to be a greaser but they wouldn't have him because he was a runt who mouthed-off too much and had a compulsive propensity for stretching the truth. In fact, he could barely utter a sentence without exaggerating half way through it. Kevin's father was an alcoholic. Never had any money. Kevin, however, was resourceful and always managed to get neat things. Cars, motorcycles, guns...everything the other guys wished they had."

"Joe befriended Kevin, and their little pack took him in as one of their own. Overnight, Kevin was transformed from a hodad, into a surfer. No one, however, could recall Kevin ever having contact with water (salt or otherwise)."

"One August afternoon, during the summer of 1960, Kevin made the deal of his lifetime. He had managed to trade a case of Rainier Ale for a decrepit '51 Ford Woody. It was pretty thrashed. The wood was rotted and falling away and there were no seats, front or back. The driver operated the controls while perched precariously on top of a steel milk crate. Manipulating the gas pedal was a snap; however, applying the clutch or brakes would sometimes send the pilot careening backwards onto the twin sized mattress in the back. This was seldom a problem, as there was always a full crew of joy-riders to catch the driver and shove him back onto his perch."

"In addition to catching the driver and providing occasional gas money, the ever-present rear crew had another important function. Whenever the old coach would approach a hill, they were required to leap out and push. To facilitate this, the tailgate was left in the down position. This was fortuitous, however, as the gate would not stay closed anyhow. It was a snap for the ten or so free-loaders to exit out the rear, fireman-style. Pushing accomplished two things: it saved gas, and maintained precious kinetic energy. With the added *horsepower* the old wagon chugged dutifully over most hills on its way to the group's favorite Santa Lina surf breaks."

"No one had a driver's license," his dad would recount, "and jeez, the car wasn't even registered so I guess it didn't matter anyhow. However, Kevin had a learner's permit which made him the ranking driver. He wore ski goggles when he drove because there was no windshield. The only thing we cared about back then was getting from Lighthouse Point to Wild Hook, back to Cowell's Beach and a warm place to sleep at night."

Suddenly Nick's thoughts were interrupted.

"Hey, can you guys push a little faster, we're almost to the top of the hill," yelled Michael from the driver's side window.

"You'd think we're a couple of bloody camels or something!" complained AJ.

"I'm not pushing anymore!" yelled Nick angrily, "you come back here and push...I'll steer!"

"We're almost to the top," urged Michael in an odd, detached voice, "you can make it!"

Nick and AJ continued to push, expending their remaining energy. Their heads drooped between their arms. "Yeah...I'll believe that when I see it," puffed Nick.

"A bloody camel," complained AJ, "that's what he thinks we are! Bloody camels!"

Suddenly the car became light and began coasting away. When it rolled off, AJ and Nick lurched forward and tumbled down hard on the rough pavement. They quickly recovered and looked up just in time to see the sun glinting off the white competition stripe that ran the length of the red sedan. The car grew smaller as it accelerated down the hill. They looked at each other incredulously, jumped up and began running in pursuit.

The Plymouth continued to gather speed and momentum as it easily crested the next series of low hills. It literally rolled out of sight as Nick and AJ hobbled along.

Over an hour passed before they spotted a grayish form ahead. It was about a quarter mile away, at the base of a small hill. It appeared to be motionless, stalled in the middle of the road.

When the two dragged themselves up to the sedan they could see the dark outline of Michael's head in the front seat. He appeared to be napping. AJ began pounding on the hood.

"Damn it! You bloody wanker! Why didn't you wait for us!"

Michael opened his eyes, rubbed them slightly then straightened up.

"Don't be such a dork," explained Michael. "Think about it! If I had stopped the car to wait for you...then you would have had to push it all the way here. So I just let it gather speed and waited until it stopped by itself." Michael grinned broadly, "and it worked great! We coasted nearly 5 miles!"

AJ and Nick raised their eyes dejectedly toward each other. Michael was always right. No matter how screwed over they got when they took part in Michael's little schemes, he would always come out smelling like a rose. It was senseless to protest.

It was another two miles down a slight incline before they reached the crapulent old gas station. As the car rolled in, it crunched across the gravel driveway. Michael hit the brakes and slid to a stop in front of the regular pump. Nick and AJ slammed into the rear trunk lid and collapsed, totally exhausted. AJ spotted a garden hose and weaved off toward it. Nick followed closely behind.

Michael exited the car and strolled toward the attendant who stood by the open doorway of the station.

"Excuse me!" said Michael.

The attendant seemed absorbed with watching Nick and AJ at the faucet. He shifted his attention between them and Michael.

"Would you put five bucks worth in, please...and can you tell me where we are?"

Without responding, the attendant proceeded over to Michael's car and began dispensing the gas. He chewed thoughtfully on something that protruded from his right cheek.

"Masonville," he responded finally. He spat brown liquid into the gravel.

"Where's that?" asked Michael.

The attendant looked at Michael curiously, then raised his left eyebrow.

"Mason County!" he drawled.

Just then Nick and AJ appeared. They each carried candy bars and sodas.

"Thanks...you're a big help," replied Michael sarcastically to the attendant.

The attendant looked at the surfboards on the car, then observed the boys.

"Guess you boys are-a headin' for Mason Ranch...huh?"

The boys exchanged bewildered looks.

"Where's that?" asked Nick finally.

"It's here in Masonville!" replied the attendant flatly.

"Okay!" barked Nick, "so where around Masonville it it?" Michael interrupted. "You won't get anywhere with that, I already tried!" The attendant scratched his head quizzically and spat again. This time the brown juice arced upwards, struck the gravel and splashed against the car's front tire.

"Mason Ranch is about five or six miles down this road," said the attendant pointing to the main highway and then in a southward direction. He removed the nozzle from the tank.

"Old man Mason died a few years back...he was a surfin-board rider too. Used to come in here with his old Pontiac station wagon...surfin-board a-hangin out the back. Funny thing for a man of sixty-sumpin' years to be a-doin."

The attendant cleared his throat. "Anyways...when you see an old barn with a windmill next to it, make a right. Then follow the dirt road toward the sea. Ya can't miss it."

Michael thanked the attendant and handed over the five dollar bill. He turned to Nick and AJ.

"Mason," remarked Michael thoughtfully, "where have I heard that name before?"

Mason Ranch

The car's factory-rally suspension absorbed the numerous potholes as Michael sped down the dirt road. Soon they passed a faded, gray-green sign that read *Mason Ranch*. Within moments the azure blue of the Pacific began to crest the horizon. As they topped a small rise they could see the golden expanse of several miles of sand beach. They drove down a narrow dirt driveway lined with willow trees, until they came to an old dilapidated ranch house. A run-down barn stood adjacent to the house. The structure leaned a full thirty degrees and appeared to be in imminent danger of collapsing.

Michael parked the car facing the ocean and they all sat staring out to sea. It was a deserted beach for as far as the eye could see, with a backdrop of rolling sienna grass covered hills and grazing cows.

"Where the hell are we?" asked AJ.

"Hell," replied Michael, "Mason Ranch, I guess. But hey, there are some waves out there!"

The waves that Michael was talking about were large and unfriendly-looking. They were the common kind that swept over jagged reefs and crashed into angry looking rocks along hundreds of miles of California coastline. Down the beach, however, about two hundred yards Michael had spotted a well defined wedge with a steep, bowling right. It looked rideable.

Nick glanced at Michael. "Well, now what?" he quizzed.

Michael looked down the white sand beach.

"Hey guys...wanna go surf that peak and see what it's like?".

"Looks too big and unrideable to me," replied AJ.

"We could surf, then camp here tonight!" suggested Michael cheerfully. He climbed out of the car.

"It's pretty enough!" said AJ. "But what are we supposed to eat?"

"I still have a few candy bars left," replied Michael.

AJ and Nick looked at each other and shrugged as if they had given up completely.

The boys quickly changed into their wetsuits and strolled up the beach. They entered the cold water tentatively, then began the strenuous paddle out. It was tough going and proved to be very exhausting to both AJ and Nick. It was ten minutes before they managed to make it out to the line-up, where Michael sat waiting. They watched the large waves steam in. As was usually the case when surfing a strange spot, the waves proved to be much larger and ominous than they had appeared to be from the beach.

"These waves are bloody crazy, mate," exclaimed AJ to Michael. "You're not really serious about surfing these things, are you? Look at the bloody rocks on the inside. Its bloody suicide!"

"He's right, Michael," added Nick. "These are not friendly waves...maybe we should just go on in."

Michael had become subdued. He was quietly studying each approaching wave. Watching as they would jack-up, hit the rock reef, throw out, then crack noisily against the unyielding bottom.

"You guys can go ahead...I've got a hunch that these waves are rideable," he replied without turning toward them. Michael had pulled within himself, very much like when he practiced karate. He continued watching and analyzing each wave. He imagined himself taking off, dropping in and riding. It was much like what he did during a tournament, when he would mentally size up an opponent before a sparring match. Strangely, he felt the need to challenge himself as he calmly appraised his chances of survival. He felt the familiar butterflies in his stomach. Some frightening, inner impulse was compelling him to face this new challenge. He recalled the huge wave in his strange, recurring dream. He imagined that Nick's dad had faced much worse when he surfed the huge waves of Maverick's.

Michael turned and looked toward the beach. He watched his friends walk briskly up the long sand beach toward the farm house. He returned his attention to the sea. A large set of waves approached.

"Must be seven or eight waves in that set," he thought. "Got to go for it."

He paddled quickly toward the reef and moved into position to catch the third wave of the set. The sun gleamed brightly from the west and illuminated the wave's face. He halted his board, rotated, went prone and began to paddle. The wave pitched up suddenly as it hit the outer reef. Michael instinctively stopped paddling as he felt gravity take over and pull him down. The wave abruptly leaped up to well overhead as Michael jumped to his feet and continued his descent. The water rushed past beneath his board as he was swept down and across the more shallow section of the reef. Without warning the wave leapt up again.

It became concave and fell noiselessly over him. All light became blotted out as he was engulfed and pulled immediately over the falls. He went down hard, compressed under tons of cold, unyielding turbulence.

Michael was not an accomplished big wave rider by any stretch of the imagination and was definitely not enjoying his underwater episode. Normally, he confined himself to the easy breaks around Santa Lina. Never before had he any desire to prove himself in such big waves. Never before today.

After eight long seconds of fighting for survival in the cold dark water, he managed to claw his way to the surface. Luckily, he had managed to evade the hard rock bottom.

"Pfooo!"

He expelled the spent air from his lungs and sucked in a fresh breath. In less than a heartbeat another wall of white water charged down upon him. He dove deep and felt his surf leash straining as it stretched out to its maximum length. He prayed that it would not break. Being stranded out there would be dangerous and the rip on the inside was much too strong to swim through. Michael was trapped in what surfers lovingly refer to as, "the Pit." He was stuck between the path of an advancing set of unyielding waves and the dangerous rocks and rip on the inside. A situation like this could quickly drain even a well-trained big wave rider of precious energy. He surfaced again and struggled back onto his board. Suddenly, he noticed something moving out of the corner of his eye. He glanced southward and about fifty yards away was another surfer. He was waving frantically for Michael to paddle his way. Michael struggled momentarily in the turbulence then began to paddle with all his might in the other surfer's direction. He was relieved when he realized that he had out-paddled the next wall of white water. The kinetic force of his paddling carried him forward as he sailed into the deeper waters of the adjacent channel. He stopped within five feet of the stranger. The man addressed Michael in a friendly tone.

"Hello, partner!"

He was an older man with a dark tan. Michael guessed that he must be in his sixties. He wore graying hair long and bushy mutton-chop sideburns and sat astride an old longboard of some kind. The board looked familiar.

Michael continued to stare. His mouth remained ajar as he panted in exhaustion and confusion. He was struggling to determine where this strange man could have come from.

"I noticed you was havin' some problems there," said the man. "Would you mind some advice?"

"No...not at all," replied Michael.

The old man spun the board around.

"Just watch me then. It's a lot easier than a bunch of lip flappin.'"

As he turned, Michael caught a glimpse of the sticker at the rear of the surfboard. It was a classic Dale Velzy pop-out. The same kind of surfboard that Joe Giovani used to ride! The surfboard was nine feet, nine inches in length. As the man moved into position he turned-turtle under a critical wave, exposing the distinctive laminated wood rainbow fin, securely glassed and beaded to the very end of the tailblock. The board was designed specifically for fast-breaking critical point-break surf. Michael recalled Joe ripping on eight-foot plus days at Rincon.

Dale Velzy invented the pop-out surfboard manufacturing method and this board was one of his best models. To build a pop-out, foam was blown into a specially prepared cement mold. After the foam had set-up the mold was split and the surfboard extracted. It was pretty much in its final form with foam, glass and resin fused together. Next, the laminated wood fin was glassed on, and very often, Velzy would add a little colored resin paneling. Finally, a thin gloss coat was applied and after a brief rub-out, it was ready for the water. This board was a classic Velzy shape with medium egg rails and just a little belly on the bottom to make it forgiving. The parallel rails and gentle rocker flowed back to a modest six inch tail block at one end and a softly rounded nose at the other. It was not, however, the kind of surfboard that Michael would expect to see ridden at a treacherous reef break like this.

Michael watched as the man paddled effortlessly into an approaching wave, turned the board and paddled. As he dropped to the bottom of the double overhead wave, he eased the board around and tucked in just as the wave hit the reef. Just as with Michael, the wave jacked-up and closed over him. A second later, however, he came popping out of a deep barrel, whooping loudly. Then he swung the longboard easily around and kicked out. Michael could not believe his eyes. The guy surfed that old tanker as well as any hot Santa Lina longboarder he had ever seen. He sat and watched him catch one incredible ride after another.

Soon the man waved for Michael to paddle over. He and Michael shared waves for the next hour. Suddenly, the man turned north and began paddling away.

"Gotta go bud," he shouted over his shoulder. "Nice surfin' with ya!"

"Wait," cried Michael, "I didn't catch your name!" The man stopped and turned around. "My friends call me Mase," he yelled. "And, kid, keep on searchin'...you're almost there!"

Then he reeled around and paddled away. Michael watched him disappear behind some breaking waves, into the blinding red sunset.

Michael caught one last wave. He rode the whitewater over the rip and in to shore. As he walked up the steep beach he could see that AJ and Nick had build a large campfire. He hurried over, changed quickly and went to the fire to warm himself up.

"How was the surf, dude?" asked Nick.

"Saw ya get some dynamite rides, yer old bloke," added AJ.

Michael warmed his back-side on the roaring fire.

"Yeah, I had a great time. Those waves were fun once you got the hang of it. That old guy, Mase, showed me how to ride 'em."

AJ and Nick stared at each other incredulously. "Who's this Mase bloke?" asked AJ.

Michael looked from AJ to Nick. He smiled nervously and shook his head.

"The guy that I was surfing with out there...the old guy. He was riding an old Velzy pop-out like your dad had, Nick!"

Nick looked seriously at his friend. "We didn't see anyone out there but you, bud!"

Michael continued to shake his head. His smile transformed from amusement to twisted irony.

"Yeah...right! You guys are trying to get back at me for this afternoon, right? Don't bullshit me!"

Michael turned abruptly and walked away from the fire. He went to the driver's side of the car, reached in and got his sleeping bag from the back.

Nick and AJ looked at each other once again. Something very strange was taking place in their lives and they were becoming tired and shaken.

It was eleven o-clock when the boys finally fell to sleep. They lay scattered around the campfire.

Michael slept on the opposite side of the fire from Nick and AJ. The faint sound of ancient Hawaiian music and human voices mixed with the murmur of the breaking waves were barely audible inside Michael's head. The sounds amplified, growing progressively louder and more distinct. Michael was having his recurring dream. In the dream he saw Duke Kahanamoku and the three strange men. Again, the Duke stood behind them and they kneeled at his feet, each on one leg. This time, Michael scanned the group. He began with a close look at the Duke then slowly panned across the other faces. His mind's eye stopped and focused on the man to the Duke's right. This man's face looked very familiar with its longish gray hair and thick sideburns.

"It's Mase," he thought. "It's the old guy I surfed with this afternoon!" Michael's heart pounded madly. He shifted his gaze to the man with the floppy hat. The man slid back the hat, revealing his features in the light. It was Joe Giovani! Nick's father! The shock of this realization jolted him awake.

"Ahhnghh..."

Michael jerked bolt upright in his bag and sat blinking into the darkness. The soft melodic sounds slowly dissipated as the final realization struck him. The man he had surfed with that afternoon, Mase. Mase must be short for Mason...Mason Ranch! Now it was beginning to make sense. The recurring dream of a surfing Shangri-La and the spiritual entities who kept reappearing, beckoning him to join them. Had the dream implanted an inspiration deep within him; a vision of an extraordinary place and an irresistible obsession to seek it out? He recalled the first incident at *Pleasure Cafe* when he and his friends encountered the three illusive surfer entities who had conversed about a secret spot. That same night at the beach party, the three strangers had appeared again, relating great tales of surfing and spiritual camaraderie – then vanished. Michael considered that evening. Had the beach party incident imbibed him with a new, even greater sense of urgency; an irresistible impulse to embark southward on a surfing safari? If so, it was a safari that had, so far, proven to be extraordinarily eventful. It had commenced with a near brush with death on foggy Highway 1, followed by their rescue by a strange, but familiar, guardian angel-like being. An un-winged spirit who piloted an ancient surf Woody. A celestial being dispatched, apparently, to protect and watch over them as they proceeded south. Further, this eventful journey was punctuated by their running out of gas in Mason County. The very home of Mase, a central spiritual entity from Michael's recurring dream. Mase, who surfed with Michael and encouraged him to 'Keep on...you're almost there.' The same Mase who revealed himself in Michael's final dream of revelation. The dream where Michael also discovered the true identity of the man in the large brimmed straw hat. One thing, however, was still unclear. Why hadn't Joe Giovani contacted Nick directly? Was there some unrecorded spiritual ordinance preventing Joe from contacting his son directly? Or had he realized that only Michael had the deep sensitivity, spiritual strength and tenacity required to guarantee a successful journey? It was certain, however, that what was occurring was not magic! It was destiny playing out – their destiny.

Michael observed his sleeping buddies. They were good friends. They always agreed with his crazy schemes and hardly ever complained. He considered for a moment if he should wake them up and tell them about his revelations.

"Naw," he confirmed to the night. "I'll tell 'em in the morning."

Michael gazed up and down the beach. The moon illuminated the white sand and shone silvery across the water. He looked back again at Nick and AJ. The yellow campfire embers cast a warm glow over them and created eerie shadows on the side of the car behind them. Michael pulled himself out of the sleeping bag, slowly straightened up and folded his arms across his chest. He shivered slightly as he stepped away from the fire and descended the sandy incline until he reached the edge of the water. There he squatted, staring out to sea. The swell had dropped. Small waves crumbled outside creating muted flashes of whitewater in the moonlight. He hunkered there, his knees clinched against his chest, silhouetted against the ocean. His breath became slow and rhythmic. He fell into a deep sleep.

SECRET SPOT

Michael accelerated south down Ventura Highway 101, the smooth ribbed concrete road that connects San Luis Obispo with Santa Barbara and Los Angeles. He rubbed his red eyes and squinted into the early morning sunlight as it crested the foothills. He had not slept much last night. In fact, at about four AM he was startled awake as cold water from the incoming tide splashed across his legs. He returned to his sleeping bag, but couldn't get back to sleep. At that time he had again considered telling Nick and AJ about the dream and his revelations, however, after several hours of reflection, decided against it.

"They've put up with enough from me already," he had reasoned.

Besides, the incredible compulsion to continue driving south seemed to be growing more intense. He recalled the comment from Mase, "You're almost there." He could not let anything jeopardize this trip.

They cruised along next to the Pacific, observing long parallel lines of waves marching to shore. It looked like the beginning of a new west swell. Michael knew that the south coast would have some waves. AJ and Nick knew, however, that with waves there would be crowds and attitudes as well. Nevertheless, they accompanied Michael on another of his wild ideas, instead of demanding to be taken home. This time, however, they sensed the importance of Michael's obvious obsession to keep driving south.

Michael pegged the speedometer at seventy miles-per-hour as the old car hummed along reliably. The wonderful sage colored hills, reacting to early showers, had taken on Kelly green highlights. Clumps of live oaks clung to their windward slopes, looking like tufts of fur on the back of gigantic sleeping bison. They rolled down the windows and allowed the warm sage scented breeze to circulate through the car. California's natural perfume had its invigorating effect on them. They began to exchange lively conversation.

"Boy, these past few weeks have been bloody unusual," said AJ.

"Yeah...and weird, too," added Nick.

"All that's going to change," said Michael with confidence. "Trust me."

Four hours later they rounded the majestic point at Port Hueneme. As they sped along the Pacific Coast Highway they beheld the spectacular stretch of highway that serpentined its way to Malibu and points beyond. Michael began to chatter excitedly.

"Here it is, guys...the most beautiful coastline in the world. The Pacific Coast Highway!"

They roared ahead, skimming along at near sea level. Nick glanced to the south. There on the horizon just over the low foothills, a bank of fog drooped down over the rolling hills, peppered with the homes and mansions of the wealthy of Los Angeles County. Finally, they topped the last rise and rounded the last curve. Below them lay the glimmering jewel of the south coast. They were about to pass Malibu Beach. Within moments they had an unfettered view of a typically crowded Malibu beach day. There were small waves and hundreds of surfboards in the water. Michael pulled the Plymouth over to the curb.

"Here it is you guys, Malibu Beach, the soul of surfing," explained Michael. "Nicky, remember where your dad taught us how to surf? It was Malibu. Some of the best times we've ever had surfing have been at Malibu! Your dad loved Malibu, Nicky.'"

"No way, mates!" groaned AJ from the back seat. "I'm not going out in that bloody mess...I'd rather sit in the bloody car and listen to the radio!"

Yeah," said Nick. "It's crowded; that fog bank is heading our way and there aren't any waves."

Michael seemed unaffected by their remarks. He sat bolt upright behind the wheel. His eyes searched through the thin mist that slowly snaked down along the sunny beach.

"Mikey, me bonzer bloke," replied AJ with a smile. "This place is packed to the hilt and there's no way I'm gonna fight through that mess!"

It was true. From their point of view, the beach and water were packed with sun worshipers and surfers of every variety.

Michael seemed mesmerized and remained transfixed by something that only he seemed able to perceive. He steadied himself and addressed his friends.

"Please...trust me this last time, you guys," he said reassuringly. "We need to park and get down there!"

Nick recalled his own solemn vow to "never let Michael do it to him again".

"Aw, jeez Michael!" pleaded Nick. "Have mercy on us for crying out loud!"

Michael turned tawny eyes toward Nick.

"Nicky, please, just trust me one last time! Honestly, I know what I'm doing!"

Nick raised his eyebrows. Was his friend losing his mind? He decided to humor him, maybe surfing would calm him down.

"Okay...lets go surf the crap," said Nick.

Michael smiled and backed the car into a parking spot on the busy highway. He switched off the ignition.

AJ and Nick muttered expletives quietly as Michael sprang from the car and removed the boards from the roof racks. Then he swung back into the front seat, grabbed a towel and began changing into his wetsuit. AJ and Nick reluctantly followed his example.

Soon the three were descending the dirt bank that supports the highway on one side and blends with the white sand beach on the other. Once reaching the bottom of the grade, it was another two hundred yards to the water's edge.

They trudged along together, threading through hoards of sunbathers. Most were coated with oil that glistened in the hot sun. Heatwaves radiated from the surface of the expansive sand beach. Michael plopped down about one hundred yards from the water. Nick and AJ dropped their surfboards and hunkered down behind him. They watched the small waves roll into shore. Each wave had at least three surfers riding.

"Oh well, we could go out and goof around!" said Nick.

"Yeah, replied AJ, "might be fun at that. At least we could get in a good paddle!"

Michael sat with his gaze fixed upon something ahead in the water. Something barely visible through the thin mist hanging above the sea. He turned to his friends to ask them if they could see it. They squatted side-by-side behind him. They looked tired and hungry, but their expressions were a mix of devotion and understanding. As he observed his buddies, he was once again struck with the realization that he was very fortunate. Not many people were lucky enough to have good friends like Nick and AJ. It didn't really matter where the three of them surfed, or whether it was crappy or crowded. What really mattered was being able to surf together. That's what the sport of surfing was really about, just like he saw in his dream. Sharing waves and good times with your friends was most important. Even more important than seeking out some secret surfing Shangri-La.

At that moment the large fog bank swirled overhead as if it were being propelled by an invisible lofty jet stream. Then another eddy of wind blasted down from above and drove the thick billowing gray cloud downward, like a rain-swollen river pouring over the edge of a towering waterfall. The mist swirled and poured across the road and down the bank toward the beach. The boy's hair began to whip around as a warmer breeze then gusted in from the south. It drove headlong into the advancing wall and created a vortex that spun the mist into a spiraling iridescent tunnel. The tunnel reached from where the boys were, across the blistering sand and down to the water's edge. Golden yellow light streamed from the tunnel's opening, illuminating the three as they stood watching in astonishment.

"Whoo–hooo...you guys," screamed Michael,"look at that!"

"Yeah...I see it," said AJ. "This is bloody insane!"

As they peered through the ethereal tunnel, they could see the ocean out the other end. The sea was pulsating with an eerie green color, and looked uninhabited except for rows of rolling swells.

AJ swallowed hard. "Are you blokes sure that we should go through with this? It's bloody insane, you know!"

"It'll be okay AJ, trust me," assured Michael as he entered the tunnel and led the way. Nick and AJ followed close behind.

As they moved along it became soundless except for the intensifying roar of the waves breaking ahead.

Nick felt his knees wobble weakly as he pressed close to Michael. He gazed from side-to-side, his mouth agape as he moved forward.

Through the translucent tunnel wall he could see the hundreds of surfers, tourists and sun bathers. But ahead, through the tunnel exit there was only an empty, intensely bright pearl white sand beach and the sea. The sand inside the tunnel squeaked beneath their bare feet, as if they were the first to ever walk over its surface.

They continued along apprehensively, their hearts pounding in anticipation of what they might soon find. As they emerged from the hazy womb-like enclosure, they were greeted by a melodious mix of Hawaiian guitar and human voices, chanting ancient Island ballads. Above the music was the roar of the surf.

The boys were dumbstruck. They stood and contemplated perfect four to five foot surf as it marched shoreward. Nick gazed up and down the deserted pristine beach. He turned back toward the Pacific Coast Highway. To his amazement, the once busy highway had been replaced by a deserted, narrow, two-lane road. In addition, the Malibu pier had changed. It was smaller, with only a lone shack at its end.

From outside in the line-up came the raucous clamor of deep male voices. Visible on the horizon were three lone surfers. Each sat astride antique longboards. Beautiful glassy swells rolled in, lifting them gently as they passed. It was the three strange men. The same three strangers they had encountered time after time. The men from Michael's dream.

The boys watched as the men began surfing, riding wave after wave, hooting each other on. Suddenly their antics were interrupted by a tall figure who surfed through their midst from far outside. It was The Duke. He slid past them, riding majestically on an ancient redwood Hot Curl surfboard. He cruised along gracefully on a perfect six foot wave. The bright sun seemed to flash across his broad smile.

The boys stood mesmerized; both excited and paralyzed. Nick watched one of the men intently. Suddenly his eyes began welling with tears.

"Dad!" he yelled as he waved frantically to the figure seated on the familiar old Velzy longboard. His father removed his hat and began waving back.

"Come on, Nicky!" exclaimed Joe as he flapped his big straw hat over his head. "Let's get some waves!"

The other men now hooted excitedly and called out for the boys to join them. Michael looked at Nick's tear streaked face, then at AJ.

"The Secret Spot..." whispered Michael.

The boys entered the water and began a paddle race out to the line-up.

Now, the misty gateway began to dissipate and gently lift away. It was carried aloft by a warm flower scented breeze into the deep blue sky. The strange and wonderful scene began to slowly fade from view. It was replaced by a log jam of surfers scurrying about, fighting to get a wave to themselves. Up and down the beach for as far as you could see, hundreds of people littered the worn, stained sand of Malibu Beach. The heavy, musky smell of suntan oiled bodies mixed with the fertile scent of the sea and permeated the warm summer air.

Secret Spot

159

Sanctuary of Terror

By Michael E. DeGregorio

Sanctuary of Terror is a tale of greed and espionage as a corrupt business man named Lockwood erects a sea park in a small town on the Carmel coast. He builds over a known seismic activity zone, then fills the preserve with large sea mammals, including some of the most dangerous sea creatures in existence.

The park is a big hit, however, mother nature and an angry killer whale collaborate to wreak havoc on the small Monterey Bay town. To complicate matters, a well organized band of third-world militia have infiltrated the local environmental protection organization and transformed the sanctuary into an oasis for their covert military intelligence activities.

Terror and a fight to the death ensue as the fate of United States ocean habitats hang in the balance. The young hero, Jake, saves the day when he takes on the enemy forces, Lockwood and a deadly Killer Whale named Moby.

WE DELIVER!

Order "Secret Spot" or "Thunder Bay" by using the handy ordering information at the bottom of this page.

"Secret Spot" $14.95

"Thunder Bay" $14.95

Mr./Mrs._____

Address_____

City/State_____Zip_____

Please send me the item(s) I have checked above. I am enclosing $_____ (plus $4.95 shipping and handling for each item ordered) Send check or money order, cash or COD's please, to:

**DeGregorio Productions
394 Bahr Drive,
Ben Lomond, CA. 95005
Phone/FAX (408) 335-0229**

Please allow four to six weeks for delivery.